NUR

'I've heard the doctor in charge is a tyrant . . .' Nurse Bryony Sellers remarks to a handsome stranger. But soon after starting work at the Highfields Nursing Home in Cornwall she finds herself wishing she had never been so indiscreet!

Books you will enjoy
in our Doctor–Nurse series

NURSE OVERBOARD by Meg Wisgate
EMERGENCY NURSE by Grace Read
DOCTORS IN DISPUTE by Jean Evans
WRONG DOCTOR JOHN by Kate Starr
AUSTRIAN INTERLUDE by Lee Stafford
SECOND CHANCE AT LOVE by Zara Holman
TRIO OF DOCTORS by Lindsay Hicks
CASSANDRA BY CHANCE by Betty Neels
SURGEON IN DANGER by Kate Ashton
VENETIAN DOCTOR by Elspeth O'Brien
IN THE NAME OF LOVE by Hazel Fisher
DEAR DOCTOR MARCUS by Barbara Perkins
RAINBOW SUMMER by Sarah Franklin
SOLO SURGEON by Lynne Collins
NEW DOCTOR AT THE BORONIA by Lilian Darcy
HEALERS OF THE NIGHT by Anne Vinton
THE RETURN OF DR BORIS by Lisa Cooper
DOCTOR IN NEW GUINEA by Dana James
PARIS NURSE by Margaret Barker
ROSES FOR CHRISTMAS by Betty Neels
NURSE IN BERMUDA by Helen Upshall
YESTERDAY'S LOVE by Judith Worthy
THE FAITHFUL FAILURE by Kate Norway

NURSE BRYONY

BY

RHONA TREZISE

MILLS & BOON LIMITED
London · Sydney · Toronto

*First published in Great Britain 1984
by Mills & Boon Limited, 15–16 Brook's Mews,
London W1A 1DR*

ISBN 0 263 74544 9

Set in 11 on 12½ pt Linotron Times
03/0184

*Photoset by Rowland Phototypesetting Ltd
Bury St Edmunds, Suffolk
Made and printed in Great Britain by
Richard Clay (The Chaucer Press) Ltd
Bungay, Suffolk*

CHAPTER ONE

AFTER hours of travelling, the train rumbled triumphantly over the Tamar bridge into Cornwall. Tables were littered with sugar and crumbs and half-eaten sandwiches resting on torn plastic. Paper mugs that had held tea or coffee stood in spilt liquid. But Bryony did not notice the mess for she was reading and re-reading a newspaper cutting.

Her normally light grey eyes were dark with emotion, her knuckles like polished bones in her clenched fists. For several moments she sat quite still, seeming not to breathe, then, with a characteristic gesture she raised her chin defiantly and tossed her short fair hair off her forehead. She hesitated only briefly before she crushed the cutting into a ball, held it tightly for a moment, then, as one of the staff from the restaurant car approached with his litter-bin, threw it on the table and watched as it was whisked away. She gave a short, sharp sigh. That was the end of that. She was starting a new life.

Nevertheless she touched the third finger of her left hand as if she were searching for the engagement ring that Nick had given her. Nick Cole with his laughing eyes, his quick sense of humour. She should have been Mrs Cole by now. Remembering, her heart filled with breath-catching pain at the loss, the failure and her sense of humiliation. She had been so sure that he loved her, they had got on so well together, laughed at the same things—chiefly his cartoons, but even at the amusing pictures he had painted of how desperately hard-up they would be when they were married. For a cartoonist, unless he was at the top of his profession, made only a precarious living. But they were in love and agreed that they could cheerfully face any hardships together.

It was after the wedding date was fixed and the invitations had been sent out that he began to get moody and frequently made excuses not to see her. Gradually it seemed they could find nothing to laugh at and one night he told her, while studiously avoiding her eyes, that he loved her too much to marry her when he had so little to offer. She had wept bitterly and told him that she only wanted him, but she could not persuade him to change his mind. To her infinite shame a week or two later she had seen a paragraph in the *Telegraph* which announced the engagement of Nick Cole to Pamela Cutts, the only daughter of Sir Michael Cutts who was the head of a well-known firm of publishers.

'Are you on holiday?'

Bryony gave a start of surprise and looked for the first time at the rosy-cheeked woman who had addressed her. She shook her head.

'No such luck. I'm going to Polwithy to work.'

'To work?' The woman spoke in a sing-song

Cornish voice. 'You do surprise me. There's a lot of unemployment down that way. I shouldn't have thought there was any openings for people from up the country.'

Once again Bryony congratulated herself on having got this job. She had wanted to move as far away from London, and her friends and relations as possible, the sympathy and the perpetual memories were too much to bear. It was early summer and brochures of Cornwall painted alluring pictures, but she might have to wait a lifetime before a vacancy occurred in one of the hospitals there, she discovered when she made enquiries. Then she saw in a very select magazine that a nurse was required in Highfields Nursing Home, Polwithy, Cornwall. The thought of changing from a National Health hospital to a private Nursing Home did not really appeal to her, for she knew and liked the large, busy wards, the variety of patients from all walks of life and the camaraderie of the staff and the medical students. But with increased depression her longing to get away persuaded her to apply for the post and to her surprise she got it.

Bryony realised that the woman was still looking at her questioningly.

'I'm a nurse,' she said.

'Oh yes? From up London?'

'Yes. From St Stephen's.'

'I've been to London,' the woman said proudly. 'I went up to visit my nephew. He lives at Beckenham, you'd know that I expect.'

Bryony shook her head. 'No, I don't know that part of London at all.'

'Well I suppose it was nice enough. He took me all round, showed me everything, the Houses of Parliament and Westminster Abbey and Madame Tussaud's. His wife took me to the big stores. Very kind they were and it was all very interesting, but I couldn't live there. No. I like Cornwall and don't want to live nowhere else.'

Bryony smiled. 'Do you know Polwithy?'

'Polwithy? Yes, it's quite near where I live. Are you going to work at the hospital there?'

'No. unfortunately I couldn't get in there. I'm going to Highfields Nursing Home.' Bryony looked at the woman with a question in her eyes.

She gave a short laugh. 'My soul! I'm surprised you haven't got to pay just to look at that place. What they charge is nobody's business! When I heard it frightened me! Still, I suppose some people have got the money and can afford to pay. There are a lot of very wealthy people in Cornwall. I'd rather spend my money on something else and go in the General if I had to.'

Bryony agreed with the woman whole-heartedly. 'I do hope I am going to like it there,' she said.

'I daresay you'll like it all right, it's a handsome looking place and they've got everything of the latest I'm sure. But the doctor in charge there—the head chap—well he isn't easy to work for so I've heard. The reason I know is my sister's youngest girl helped out in the kitchen for a time but she soon left, said she couldn't stand it. She said when he came in it was just as if Royalty had arrived, everything had to be just so and God help you if it wasn't. He used to go in the kitchen and everywhere and make sure everything was as he wanted it.'

'Which doctor is that, I wonder? There was a Dr Crosland on the notepaper heading . . .'

'That's right, that's him. Dr Crosland. Rolling in money, and no wonder.'

Bryony felt a wave of distaste. Here was another man who put money before everything else. In her opinion there was something very wrong in making money from people's ill-health. Well, no matter. She was going to Highfields to do a job which she was glad to have got, and would probably have little or no contact with this Dr Crosland. If she did and he made things too unpleasant she would move elsewhere as soon as she was able.

The woman spoke of her family and of her trip to London, Bryony gave monosyllabic replies which seemed all that was required of her. She was enjoying looking at the scenery, the lush green fields, the sheep and the cattle, and later, the glimpse of the sea.

'Lovely, isn't it?' the woman said as a pyramid of rocks and trees topped by a castle came into view.

'Is that St Michael's Mount?' Bryony asked, her face pressed against the window to get a better view.

'Yes, that's right. That's Lord St Levan's home—

it belongs to the National Trust now. You want to go over and see it some time. There's a causeway and you can walk across when the tide is out or take a ferry if it isn't. You're only allowed in the castle on certain days, you want to enquire about that. No point in going over there just to walk around the harbour and the few cottages, there's nothing else there.'

'It must be a stiff climb to the top,' Bryony suggested.

'That's true enough. I wouldn't want to do it now but a young lady of your age shouldn't have no trouble. There's a proper path that winds around so it isn't as bad as it looks.'

The train now ran alongside the beach and passengers began lifting their luggage from the racks and standing expectantly by the doors. It slid into the station and with a sigh of relief shuddered to a stop as if tired after the long journey. Now that Bryony had reached her destination she felt apprehensive and very much alone. The woman had lost interest in her travelling companion and with barely a nod of farewell took her place in the queue waiting to step down on to the platform. Bryony waited until all the passengers had left, for she was in no hurry to start this new life. At last she picked up her suitcase and made her way out of the exit which led to the bus terminus and taxi rank.

Beyond the station yard was a large car-park and then the harbour, full of brightly coloured boats, but in the yard there were no taxis. Bryony asked a bus driver if he was going in her direction but he said a bus had just left and there would not be another for an hour. A porter told her that all the taxis had been taken and he doubted if they would return until the next train was due, later in the evening.

She put her suitcase on the pavement and wondered what to do next. A sleek, expensive car slid to a stop nearby and a young, good-looking man climbed out and went into the station. After a few minutes he returned carrying a neat parcel. As he was about to get into the car he changed his mind and walked across to the porter.

'Thanks for the fish, Bert, it was delicious,' he said in a warm, cultured voice.

The porter touched his hat and moved towards him. 'You're more than welcome, sir.'

They continued to chat and Bryony watched them, fascinated by the man's appearance. He reminded her vividly of a lion with his strong, lithe shoulders, chestnut-coloured hair, a lock of which fell over his forehead, his strong, straight nose and proud, watchful eyes. She had not realised that she was staring at him until she saw that the men seemed to be talking about her. Immediately she turned aside and looked in the opposite direction.

'You're in luck, Miss,' a voice beside her said. 'The gentleman says he'll give you a lift to wherever you want to go.' He picked up her case.

'Oh no—no thank you. I—I'll wait for a taxi or a bus . . .' she stammered.

A short blast of a car horn made her turn involuntarily. The man, now in the driving seat, beckoned to her with an imperious forefinger. Before she could protest further the porter had carried her case across and put it on the back seat.

The driver opened the passenger door. 'Where can I drop you?' His voice was rich and deep but decidedly distant.

'It is really very kind of you, but there is no need—I—' She sat uncomfortably on the edge of the seat.

Not in a million years would she have accepted a lift from a stranger in London, but here it seemed different, especially as the porter knew him.

'I asked where I could drop you,' he said with a hint of impatience.

'Oh—yes—I'm sorry. It's—a boarding-house—I've got a card here somewhere.' She found it in her handbag and showed it to him.

He nodded. 'Right.'

He reversed the car and turning left drove along the quay. The harbour was filled with boats of all sizes from sailing-boats to big merchant ships, and on the other side of the road were tall shabby warehouses bordering the dry dock.

But Bryony was more interested in the man sitting beside her. He was expensively dressed in tweeds with leather shoes and belt. His hands, which rested lightly on the steering-wheel, were firm and capable and the nails well-manicured. He was extremely handsome. Nick had been good-looking too, in a totally different way, with more delicate features, laughing blue eyes that crinkled at the corners and hair that curled into the back of his neck. But what were looks? They were just a trick of Nature, something you were born with, a mask to cover the personality behind it. At the thought of Nick her muscles tensed and she turned aside to blot out the memory and concentrate on the scenery—St Michael's Mount now way out in the bay, the semi-circular coastline of fields and cliffs and, close by, people sitting in deck-chairs on the esplanade.

Suddenly she remembered her manners. 'I do hope that I'm not taking you out of your way,' she said politely.

'Nowhere is far out of my way, my house is fairly central.' He sounded slightly bored and she felt she was being a nuisance nevertheless.

'I expected to get a taxi,' she said, in self-justification.

'You have to make a dash for them when the train gets in. They are soon snapped up and taxi-drivers have no need to wait for late-comers.'

'So that is why everyone was champing at the bit beside the doors, I wondered why they seemed so anxious to get out. I hung around because I wasn't in any hurry. Oh well, I'll know better another time. Oh look!' Bryony twisted around to peer out through his window. 'Highfields Nursing Home. What a lovely position overlooking the sea front. It does look nice.'

His eyebrows arched. 'Are you contemplating being taken ill? You look extremely healthy to me.'

'Oh no,' she laughed. 'And if I were I couldn't possibly afford to go there. They say it costs the earth! But I'm going to work there,' she added proudly.

He glanced down at her and with a sudden thrill she saw that his eyes were magnificent. They too resembled a lion's. They were a tawny yellow and fringed with thick, curling lashes.

'Are you a nurse?' he asked.

'Yes. I have been working at St Stephen's in London and it will be a tremendous change going to a place like Highfields. But I'm lucky to have got there.'

He turned down a side street. 'This is the road you want.' He drove slowly, then stopped. 'And here is Harbour View.' He smiled sardonically. 'That is poetic licence. The only view from here is of the house opposite.'

He took her suitcase from the back seat and climbing out, opened the door for Bryony. She had not realised that he was so tall, well over six feet, and she had to tilt her head back to look up at him and thank him.

He acknowledged her with a brief nod then carried her case to the front door of the house.

'Goodbye. I hope you will be happy at Highfields.'

'Thank you, so do I. But it won't be all honey. I've heard that the doctor in charge is a tyrant, he thinks he is Royalty and almost expects you to curtsey to him when he passes! He'll be lucky,' she ended with a laugh.

His tawny eyes were inscrutable as he stared at her for several seconds. Then, at the sound of someone walking along the hall he turned away.

'It seems as if the poor man might be in for a tough time,' he said smoothly and returned to his car.

The door was opened by a short, plump woman with alert brown eyes and round, sun-tanned cheeks who spoke with a slightly Cornish accent, she introduced herself as Mrs Rosewall.

'And you'll be Nurse Sellers. Do come in.'

She ushered Bryony into a square hall with an open fireplace, a relic of days gone by when coal fires were used to heat the house. Now it held an earthenware jar of bulrushes and grasses.

After the usual preliminaries, discussing the weather and the journey, she said,

'I expect you'd like a wash and to get some of your things unpacked. I'll show you to your room.'

It was a large, clean bedroom furnished with heavy, old-fashioned furniture, certainly not the flimsy kind of wardrobe which you could tip over yourself as had happened to a nurse in the hostel at St Stephen's.

'I hope you'll find the bed comfortable. Let me know if you haven't got enough blankets. I've put you an armchair here in case you want to be on your own, but you are very welcome to sit with us and watch the television any time you like,' she said with a kindly smile.

'Thank you very much, Mrs Rosewall. Have you any other boarders besides me?'

'No. Janice—that's my daughter, she works in the Town Hall—and I, are here on our own most of the time. My husband is in the Merchant Navy and is away for months at a time. It could be lonely but I'm pretty used to it now. Well, I'll leave you to get yourself sorted out. Supper won't be long. I'll ring when it's ready. That'll be when Janice gets home.'

When Bryony had washed and changed into a pair of jeans and a sweater, and had unpacked her suitcase and put away her clothes, she went over to the window and parted the nylon curtains to look out on to the garden. But she scarcely saw the strip of grass bordered by sweet-smelling wallflowers and fruit bushes and palm trees, for unpacking the clothes she had bought for her trousseau had brought back the memory of Nick and her loss, and she felt completely empty. She had thrown away the newspaper cutting. How naïve of her to believe that in doing so she could blot out her memories.

She had known that he had met Pamela Cutts at a literary luncheon because he had casually mentioned it. It was soon afterwards that for no apparent reason he had become cooler towards her and had broken appointments for quite trivial reasons. She had been too blindly in love to see the connection. Then she had seen the announcement of his engagement, and immediately everything became clear. And understandable for lots of people. But for Nick?

Yes, definitely for Nick. With Pamela he would make the right contacts and his future as a cartoonist would look much brighter. Apart from that she was wealthy, and an occasional spell without any sales of his work would not mean disaster. Whereas Bryony only had a nurse's small salary to commend her.

But realising that did not make it easier to bear. She and Nick had been so close. But it was stupid to go on thinking about that. She had moved to another part of the country and changed to another hospital and now she must try to forget the past. But how could she?

She gripped the window-sill so hard that her knuckles shone white. Oh please—please help me, she prayed silently.

As if in immediate answer to her prayer a clear picture floated before her of the tall, brown-haired man with honey-coloured eyes, who had given her a lift, and some of her wretchedness seemed to melt away.

Before she had time to marvel at this, a bell rang in the hall and she went downstairs to supper.

CHAPTER TWO

HIGHFIELDS Nursing Home was a large granite building which occupied a site looking across the esplanade to the sea. The ground floor rooms had french doors which led on to flower-bordered terraced lawns.

Bryony climbed the flight of steps which led to the entrance and went hesitantly into the hall. It was spacious and luxuriously carpeted in a pale shade of mushroom, a colour which was echoed on the walls and formed a pleasing background for the many attractive oil paintings and water-colours, the work of local artists, and gifts from grateful patients.

After the morning freshness outside and the salty tang of the sea-air, the atmosphere was breath-catching, heavy with exotic perfumes and the scent of flowers. From behind a massive mahogany desk a middle-aged receptionist looked at Bryony with a questioning smile. On hearing her business she directed her to the Sister's office. Bryony tapped apprehensively on the door and went inside. A comfortable-looking woman in her middle forties held out a capable hand.

'Good morning, Nurse Sellers. My name is Mailer. Welcome to Highfields. Do sit down.'

She read a form which was on her desk, then looked up at Bryony again.

'I see that you have completed your third year and passed your SRN examination. Congratulations, Nurse.'

'Thank you, Sister Mailer.'

The sister toyed with a pen, turning it from side to side. 'Would you like to tell me why you resigned from St Stephen's at this quite important time in your career?'

Bryony bit her lip thoughtfully. She wanted to start here afresh and for what had gone before to be over and done with. She did not want any more sympathy, she had had enough to last her for a very long time.

She smiled apologetically. 'I am sorry, Sister, but it was for personal reasons.'

'I see. Well, it's as you wish, of course.' She took some more papers from her drawer. 'I presume you have had no experience of private nursing?'

'No, Sister. I have only been at St Stephen's.'

'Quite. Well, nursing doesn't vary in any essential way, wherever it is carried out. Actually I spent many years in a London teaching hospital so I can speak with authority. Here, the patients pay a great deal of money and expect—and get—personal attention. I think that is the chief difference.'

'Yes, I understand, Sister.'

'We do our best to make the patients feel comfortable and cared for. They each have remote control television, radio, telephone, *en suite* shower and lavatory. And bells. I must stress that when a bell rings you answer it *immediately*. Another thing—watching television for too long or talking on the phone can be exhausting and it is up to you nurses to make sure that patients are not overdoing things.'

'Do—do the patients take kindly to being told that?' Bryony asked.

Sister Mailer shook her head. 'Not always. It isn't the same as in a public ward where your word is law. So you must go carefully. It would not do for them to complain of their treatment to Dr Crosland for he would be extremely annoyed, and your days here might be numbered.'

I bet he wouldn't like it, Bryony thought mutinously, in case they discharged themselves and he lost some of his lovely lolly.

'Does Dr Crosland own the Nursing Home, Sister?'

'Not entirely, it is jointly owned by a businessman. Dr Crosland is an extremely clever doctor and a wonderfully kind man, but he doesn't suffer fools gladly. Quite rightly he wants everything in his Nursing Home to be perfect, and I like to think it is, because we all do our best. Yes, he is a perfectionist.' Her eyes became dreamy, and it was a moment or two before she asked, 'Is there anything else you wish to know?'

Bryony thought for a moment. 'Do I have my meals here, Sister?'

'Certainly, when you are on duty, and they are

excellent, I assure you. Dr Crosland is most particular about that.'

Bryony resisted the desire to raise her eyes heavenwards. If ever a man sounded objectionable it was this demi-god.

'Does he live on the premises?'

'No, he lives next door which is very convenient when he is needed in an emergency. He has rooms there where he interviews his private patients. He holds two out-patients clinics a week in Polwithy General hospital which is about a mile away, and also pays daily visits to his patients there as well as here.'

'He must be kept very busy,' Bryony said, feeling the remark was expected of her.

'Indeed, yes. Now I must tell you that this vacancy you are filling is Dr Crosland's brain-child. He has been of the opinion that a nurse is needed in a different capacity from the regular staff and you may be called upon to do various duties which may seem to have nothing to do with nursing. But believe me, they have. If a patient wants you to sit and chat or read to them or even play a game of chess or whatever with them, then that is what you must do.' Her light blue bulbous eyes travelled slowly over Bryony as if assessing her.

Blow the wretched man, Bryony thought crossly and childishly.

'But Sister, I am a trained nurse and when I applied for this post I assumed it would require my qualifications,' she said in dismay.

A slight frown creased the sister's forehead. 'I appreciate your feelings, Nurse, but you knew that this was a private nursing home when you applied for the post.'

'Yes Sister, but I didn't . . .'

'You didn't realise that things might be different from your own hospital. Well they are in many ways, but in the main they have the same objective, the welfare of the patient. In a National Health hospital it is not possible to give each patient the undivided attention he or she gets and pays for here. Dr Crosland believes that is essential.'

And what that creature says goes, Bryony thought resentfully.

Sister Mailer noticed the smouldering expression in her eyes, how their colour had changed from light grey to pewter and she compressed her lips.

'If you have second thoughts and feel the post is not for you, please say so right away so that we may make other arrangements,' she said tersely.

Bryony stared at the carpet. She had no wish to do anything other than nursing. Had she wanted to be a general dogsbody she would not have studied so hard to get her exams. She looked up at Sister Mailer with a troubled expression.

'But Sister—surely you understand my feelings?'

'In a way I do. But a nurse is one who tends the sick and that is what you would be doing. Oh, don't get me wrong. Generally speaking you would be on regular nursing duties. I am just warning you that on occasion you might well be called upon to do other things for the patients to add to their comfort. What is your answer to that?'

Bryony thought of the alternatives. Returning home to more commiseration, looking for another vacancy which might not be as good as this one, almost certainly in an area which was not so pleasant. Or staying here. After all, that did not mean she was committing herself for life. After a decent interval she could hand in her notice if it all became unbearable or if she had to put up with too much of this precious Dr Crosland and all his likes and dislikes.

She took a deep breath and opened her eyes wide. 'Thank you for putting things so plainly, Sister. I would like to stay if I may.'

Sister Mailer gave her a warm, satisfied smile. 'Good. I'm glad about that for I feel that the patients will like you. Now, I will take you to meet some of the other nurses.'

The nurse nearest in age to Bryony was a muscular girl with brawny arms and red cheeks. She was going through patients' files.

'Nurse Dyson, your cap!' Sister Mailer said reprovingly.

'Sorry Sister,' the girl said, pushing it too far in the other direction.

'That won't do, you know. See that it is correct before Dr Crosland arrives.'

'Yes Sister, I will, Sister,' she said cheerfully.

'Well, I'll leave you two together.' She turned to

Bryony with a wry smile. 'Despite her untidy appearance Nurse Dyson is very capable and will be able to tell you anything you need to know.'

When she had gone Nurse Dyson sat down heavily in an armchair and stretched her stalwart legs out before her.

'These carpets look a treat but they're hell for your legs. They're so thick-piled that you have to lift your feet up about six inches every step you take. Worn lino has its points.'

'That sounds as if you have had experience working in a general hospital,' Bryony smiled.

'True, I was at St Monica's. I haven't been here long.'

'How do you like it?' Bryony looked at her anxiously.

'Oh it's the life of Riley, luxury-wise. Mind you, I don't know that it's exactly me, I'm not quite the "refained" type that these patients prefer. I must have slipped through the Crosland net in the dark.'

'Nonsense! I expect you are a damned good nurse,' Bryony replied, feeling strongly that if she were in need of comfort that ample bosom and those strong arms would provide it.

'Thank you for those few kind words. It's quite nice here really, but I must confess that I miss the rattle of the bed-pans and the friendliness of everyone at St Monica's. Oh, the bitchiness too. Here I feel like a weed in a hot-house and sooner or later I'll be turfed out.'

Bryony looked at her doubtfully. 'What are these—duties—that we are expected to do sometimes?'

'What duties are those?' Nurse Dyson asked with joking eagerness. 'Tell me more.'

Bryony laughed at her expression. 'Well—playing games—' Before she could finish her sentence Nurse Dyson gave a whoop of delight.

'If there are any games to be played I bags I play them with Winston!'

Bryony joined in her laughter. 'I can see it isn't going to be dull with you here. Tell me, who is Winston?'

'Winston is a very dishy young man from Jamaica, where the sugar-cane grows.'

'Is he a doctor?'

'Oh no, I should say, off-hand, that he is a millionaire. How else could he stay here so long?' She rolled her eyes heavenwards.

'What's the matter with him?'

'Poor Winston went to see Dr Crosland with a badly swollen knee which was intensely painful. Do you know what the trouble was?'

'Had he injured it some time?' Bryony hazarded.

'No. There was no history of any injury, although he had had the swelling and pain before. Clue number two. He felt weak and tired and his face was pale.'

'His face was pale?' Bryony giggled.

'Yes. The lining of his mouth and eyes were pale. Now, any idea what the problem was? We were always being asked this sort of thing at St Monica's.'

'We-ell, I should say that he was anaemic and give him iron. I don't know about the knee trouble. Perhaps it was not connected to the anaemia,' Bryony suggested.

'Well, Dr Crosland admitted him . . .'

I bet he did, Bryony thought. He wasn't going to let an ailing millionaire slip through his fingers.

'And?' she prompted.

'Apparently our dear doctor had a hunch and he was right. The blood tests showed that he had sickle-cell anaemia.'

'Sickle-cell anaemia? I've never heard of it. Anyhow, surely iron is the answer?'

'Apparently not, because it builds up in the liver. He had a blood transfusion.'

Bryony nodded. 'So now he's okay?'

'It's not as simple as that.'

Oh no, silly me, Bryony thought. He needs plenty of rest at X number of pounds per day, I'll bet.

'No, he needs rest,' she said drily.

'That's right. Rest and support for the leg. He's got a plaster slab for it and will be on it for three or four weeks. After that he will be able to get around with the aid of one elbow crutch if all goes well.'

'Sickle-cell anaemia is new to me,' Bryony said.

'And to all of us ordinary mortals, I think. Apparently it is something only black people get. The test shows that the blood cells are shaped like a sickle. It's a very painful condition indeed. Poor darling, I sat beside him and talked to him like a mother, would you believe? For hours on end, on Dr Crosland's instructions! I'd like to see that happening at St Monica's. But that's what they pay for I suppose. Individual attention. Though mind you I was only too pleased to do what I could, he really was suffering.'

Bryony felt her doubts dispersing. Nurse Dyson made her realise that nurses came in many guises.

'Are there any other unusual cases here?'

'No, not at the moment. Just the usual "itises"—hepatitis, gastritis, neuritis, etcetera. Sometimes the patient complains of symptoms that don't add up to anything in particular. Most doctors put that sort of thing down to nerves, say they should snap out of it, or give them tablets. But Dr Crosland isn't like that. He will sift all the symptoms and watch the patient and if there *is* anything wrong you may depend he'll find what it is.'

'So long as they can afford to pay,' Bryony said acidly.

Nurse Dyson nodded. 'Oh they've got to do that all right.'

'What's the food like here?' Bryony remembered the thick undercooked sausages and baked beans that appeared regularly on Tuesdays in the staff canteen at St Stephen's.

'Yum-yum! I've put on a stone and a half since I've been here and I don't begrudge an ounce,' she grinned.

'I don't want to do that, I can't afford to replace my wardrobe,' Bryony said in alarm.

Nurse Dyson laughed. 'I wear smocks of varying designs and colours over extendable maternity slacks and that sees me through my meagre social life.'

She glanced at the watch which was pinned to her apron. 'I must now do my rounds. As you have been wished on me you'd better come along and make yourself known to the patients.' She looked at Bryony with raised eyebrows. 'Is my cap straight? Is my hair okay? Is there anything wrong with my appearance—anything that can be put right, I mean?' she grinned.

Bryony took the pins from her cap and set it at a different angle. 'There, that's better. As for the rest of you, it's smashing.'

They walked along the carpeted corridors and paused outside a door.

Nurse Dyson spoke quietly. 'This is the Honourable Mrs Trengwainton's room.'

'What's wrong with her?' Bryony whispered.

Nurse Dyson raised her shoulders. 'You tell me!'

The room was bathed in sunlight which shone on heavy silk curtains and cast a ray over the matching bedspread. More exotic flowers than Bryony had ever seen, apart from in a florist's shop, decorated every part of the room. On the bedside table stood a silver fruit dish which held peaches and nectarines and, merely for aesthetic reasons, it would seem, they were decorated with stems of black and green grapes. The woman sitting up in bed looked drained and petulant with tired blue eyes and well-dressed hair which was neither fair nor grey but something between the two. Her pink lace-edged pure silk bed-jacket matched her nightdress and did its best to hide the shrivelled neck. She peered across at the nurses.

'Good morning Mrs Trengwainton,' Nurse Dyson said cheerily. 'I've brought Nurse Sellers to meet you. She has just started here.'

The patient looked from Bryony's pretty fair hair, down her slim body in the pink uniform to her shapely legs, then back again to her wide-set eyes.

'Good. Dr Crosland knows that I must have young, pretty nurses around me, the other sort are so depressing.' Her eyes wandered coldly over Nurse Dyson, who popped a thermometer in her mouth.

'And how do you feel this morning?'

She moved petulantly. 'Not well at all. But then I never do.'

'Is there anything I can get you, Mrs Trengwainton?' Nurse Dyson asked, moving a vase of flowers and then replacing it.

'Yes. Prepare a peach for me, please.'

Nurse Dyson gave Bryony a side-long glance. 'Will you do that, Nurse? You can catch me up further along the corridor. Okay?'

'Okay, indeed!' Mrs Trengwainton closed her eyes disgustedly.

Bryony took a delicate china plate and a silver

fruit knife from a cabinet and cutting the fruit in quarters removed the stone.

'Is that how you like it, Mrs Trengwainton?' she asked pleasantly.

'No, I want it peeled, I can't eat the skin.'

When she had done that Bryony passed her the plate. 'Where is the fork? Am I supposed to eat it with my fingers? Really, Nurse!'

As Bryony washed her hands at the basin Mrs Trengwainton asked her if she was from London.

'Yes. From St Stephen's. It is quite a change down here.'

'I daresay. Of course I don't know anything about National Health hospitals but I should imagine they are ghastly.'

'They are really very good, the treatment is excellent and the nurses do their best for the patients,' Bryony protested.

'I suppose it depends on what one is accustomed to,' she drawled.

'Undoubtedly,' Bryony agreed, realising that Mrs Trengwainton would have been appalled if she had had to spend a night in a full ward at St Stephen's listening to the snores and belches.

'I am a very sick woman, you know.'

Bryony stood by the bedside. 'I don't suppose you would be here if you were well,' she said. 'But I am sure you are in excellent hands.'

'Indeed yes. There is nobody to compare with Dr Crosland. He seems to know exactly what I need.' She gave a swift glance at Bryony. 'You have a pleasant speaking voice, I think I will get you to read to me. Not at the moment, I am too exhausted. But later, perhaps.'

'Thank you, I should be pleased to do that,' Bryony said politely, and with a feeling of relief left her.

She was hurrying along the corridor when the lift doors opened and Sister Mailer and a tall, impeccably dressed man wearing a light grey suit, came out and walked in the direction of Mrs Trengwainton's room. Bryony suddenly recognised him as the man who had so kindly given her a lift from the station. She gave him an enchanting smile.

'Oh, hello,' she said in a delighted voice, as if she were greeting a well-liked friend.

The smile left her face as suddenly as it had appeared when she saw Sister Mailer's expression. She would not have thought that such an apparently kindly soul could look so furious. Bryony's eyes flew to her knight-errant. His face was inscrutable, there was certainly no hint of a reciprocal smile. But as he passed her one eyelid drooped. It couldn't—it couldn't possibly have been a wink, could it?

She felt a wave of embarrassment which started in her toes, rise up and flood her whole body. Her face turned scarlet as she hurried on her way. Undoubtedly he was some important visitor for Mrs Trengwainton, Lord somebody or other. But surely there was no need for them both to be so unfriendly?

She rejoined Nurse Dyson in a smaller room where a thin-faced woman was in for tests for a suspected duodenal ulcer. She was quiet and undemanding and seemed only to want to rest.

When they had completed the round and had exchanged a few pleasantries with Winston, who was a very likeable young man, they went down to the staff dining-room for coffee. Nurse Dyson brought over a plate of *petit fours* as well as the foaming coffee.

'Oh boy, is this better than a vending machine!' Bryony said, licking her lips.

'Only the best is good enough, that's the motto of Highfields,' Nurse Dyson said cheerfully.

'I'm sure I'll never know what I'm supposed to do here and what I'm not. I made the mistake of addressing a man who was with Sister Mailer. Anyone would have thought I'd committed a crime,' Bryony said ruefully.

'No wonder,' Nurse Dyson said, reaching for another *petit four*. 'One does not do that sort of thing, one doesn't!'

'I don't see why not. He gave me a lift from the station. It would have been rude to have ignored him in the circumstances.'

'Who was he, I wonder. What did he look like?'

'Like Lord Muck. Tall, well-built and beautifully dressed. With eyes like golden syrup only not so sweet. He had a sort of tic. His eyes flickered,' Bryony said thoughtfully.

Nurse Dyson spluttered over her coffee. 'You spoke to him? You'd better check on the time of your next train home.'

'What are you talking about?' Bryony frowned.

'That, my dear girl, was Dr Crosland himself.' She sketched the sign of the cross. 'One does not, under any circumstances address that gentleman unless he speaks to one first and demands an answer. That was drummed into me on my day of arrival. I don't know anything about a nervous tic—perhaps he had something in his eye.'

Bryony's mouth fell open. '*That* was Dr Crosland? But . . . but . . . whatever did I say to him when he gave me that lift?'

'I've no idea. You tell me.'

Bryony screwed up her forehead. 'It was when we passed Highfields and I said I was going to work there.' Her heart began to thump.

'There's nothing wrong with that.' Nurse Dyson took another *petit four*.

'No, but afterwards . . . I said—I wish I could remember—something about the doctor in charge here being a tyrant and expecting you to curtsey to him when you saw him!'

'So why didn't you do that?' Nurse Dyson chuckled. 'It's the truth, the whole truth and nothing but the truth.'

Bryony covered her face with her hands. 'Oh gosh! What have I done?' she groaned.

CHAPTER THREE

AFTER a fortnight Bryony began to feel more at home at Highfields, and to realise that what Sister Mailer said was true, that tending the sick was the same wherever you were. There was the usual taking of temperatures, pulse-rates, blood-pressures and medicine rounds. Drips had to be set up in just the same way, beds made, baths given and pressure points treated to prevent bed-sores.

Strangely, it was more tiring here than at St Stephen's, for it was easier and quicker to whisk around a ward full of patients than to open and close the doors of separate rooms, walk across the carpeted floors to the bedside, fetch whatever was required, speak pleasantly and listen for as long as the patient desired.

Bryony was off duty and as she passed Dr Crosland's house, she saw a little girl of about eight years of age standing by the window, staring out. She had a serious face and mouse-brown hair that hung limply to her shoulders. She looked so woebegone that Bryony instinctively stopped and smiled at her. After a moment of indecision the child smiled back, showing a gap where a second tooth had not yet come through. Bryony waved as she walked on and the little girl waved back. Poor little soul, Bryony thought, she probably has to ask her father's permission to smile.

Bryony had spent many an uncomfortable moment squirming over her gaffes with Dr Crosland. At the same time she felt indignant that he had not made himself known to her when she mentioned that she was going to work at Highfields. On the other hand, she decided crossly that he deserved to hear what other people thought of him, it would make a change from the near reverence he was accorded at Highfields. But that did not make her feel any better about it.

She would not easily forget Sister Mailer's reproving tones when she scolded her for daring to so forget herself as to address Dr Crosland when she was on duty, and in so familiar a fashion.

'But I had met him before, Sister. He very kindly gave me a lift from the station. I had no idea who he was,' she explained.

'Well you know now. What you do off duty is your own business but in Highfields you must respect his position and authority as I am sure you are well aware. I was very embarrassed and I don't think Dr Crosland liked it at all. You would do well to keep out of his sight until he has had time to overlook your conduct.'

Inevitably Bryony had seen him when he was visiting his patients, but so far she had managed to stay in the background.

'How are you settling in, Nurse?' Sister Mailer had continued in a more friendly manner.

'Quite well, thank you, Sister.'

'Good. And I am pleased to tell you that the patients have taken to you. I understand that Mrs Trengwainton would like you to read to her sometimes so that will be quite all right provided that you have no more pressing duties.'

Now, as Bryony walked across the esplanade, she wondered whether she had told the truth when she said that she had settled in, for she was tormented by doubts. Were all the patients in the fabulously expensive nursing home really ill? Were they getting any benefit from lying in bed with nothing to do but think about real or imaginary symptoms? By eating all the exotic *cordon bleu* meals when they did no exercise? When they had no fresh air but lived in a hot-house atmosphere? Was it all a great swindle that Dr Crosland and his partner was perpetrating? He was certainly a clever doctor by all accounts. Was he also a clever businessman? And which was the more important to him? She could well imagine the influence he would have over the patients. She had watched him when he spoke to them. He was gentle and kind and sympathetic and she knew that against her inclination she was as slavishly adoring of him at that moment as they were. She, however, pushed that feeling aside as soon as he had gone. But were the patients eager to stay on because they could not bear the thought of leaving him?

She paused and leaned on the railings. There were a few people bathing but she could not imagine it was a very enjoyable experience for the beach was stony and there was a cold breeze blowing. As she stared at the rippling water she wondered whether she would be here at the same time the following year. She rather doubted it. Nearly everybody at the nursing home was friendly and she had no complaints about her surroundings or the food. And yet . . . She missed the noisy wards at St Stephen's, the patients who were mostly down-to-earth East-Enders, and the camaraderie of the nurses. But most of all, how she missed Nick! He was always joking and laughing and his company had cheered her on the days when things had gone wrong. She wondered if he would be the same with Pamela Cutts. Or had he given up all the joking, the fun, for the sake of his career and the money he would earn? Money! Everything boiled down to that in the end. Would the patients at the nursing home still be confined to bed if they were poor? Would Dr Crosland still demand such deference if he were a poor man? Of course not!

She walked to the end of the esplanade, then turned back until she came to her road. How fortunate she had been in her choice of lodgings. Mrs Rosewall and Janice were super people, although Janice was very reserved. Yes, she was extremely lucky. So why did a feeling of unrest niggle away inside her?

'Had a busy day, Nurse?' Mrs Rosewall asked at supper.

Bryony thought of the days at St Stephen's when

she was rushed off her feet. There was no comparison.

'Not really, Mrs Rosewall. I lead a very calm life at Highfields.' She turned to Janice. 'How is the Town Hall treating you?'

'The same as usual. I know I'm lucky to have a job, but I'm not wildly enthusiastic about it. But you don't work for pleasure, do you? You work for money.'

'Money!' Bryony said impatiently. 'I wish it had never been invented.'

'We couldn't manage without it,' Mrs Rosewall said. 'I know I couldn't. Everything I buy in the supermarket costs two or three pence more every time—never less—and they say inflation is dropping. That's a lot of nonsense. I wish they could see what I pay out.'

The conversation turned to politics until the meal was finished, the washing up done and they were settled in front of the television.

The next morning Sister Mailer sent for Bryony. She made her way to the office with trepidation wondering what she had done wrong now. She searched her conscience but could think of nothing.

Sister Mailer looked at her with curiosity when she entered.

'Well, Nurse, I have had a request from Dr Crosland. He is taking little Wendy out for the day and would like a nurse to accompany them. We decided that you would be suitable.'

Bryony was filled with a sense of panic. 'Oh

no—I—I—surely Nurse Dyson would be more suitable?' she said desperately.

'Yes, I daresay she would. But she is needed here and you are expendable. Anyhow, as I told you when you took up this appointment, you will sometimes have to perform duties that are not strictly speaking nursing.'

'Very well, Sister,' Bryony said meekly.

'You had better not wear your uniform on this occasion so you may return home to change into something suitable. Please be back here at eleven o'clock.'

Bryony took a deep breath. 'Very well, Sister.'

'And Nurse! You should be over the moon! I am sure that you will have an enjoyable day. But not if you wear that miserable expression on your face.'

'Yes Sister. I mean no Sister.'

She walked home in a daze. She could not imagine anything more daunting than having to spend a day with the arrogant Dr Crosland and his unhappy-looking little daughter. What would she be expected to do? She wished that she had asked Sister what was wrong with the child, it would have given her an idea of what she might have to cope with.

Mrs Rosewall was out shopping so Bryony had the house to herself and she was glad. She did not feel inclined for idle conversation when she had this aura of doom hanging over her.

She stared at her clothes in the wardrobe like someone in a trance. What should she wear? She chose a light green linen suit, brushed her hair until it shone like a pale gold cap which reached just past her ears, and touched her lips and cheeks with coral blusher and her lashes with mascara. If she looked her best she would have more confidence, she decided, and she would be sorely in need of every scrap she could summon up.

On her way back to Highfields Bryony saw Dr Crosland reversing his car out of the garage of his house. She was hurrying past, her head averted, when she heard him call imperiously.

'Nurse.'

She turned reluctantly and slowly moved towards him on legs that felt weak.

He parked his car at the kerb, switched off the ignition and slid from his seat. She swallowed hard at the sight of him looking so handsome in a green velvet sports jacket and fawn slacks. He walked across to her and gave her one of the devastating smiles which she had thought were reserved for his paying patients. It served to make her feel worse than ever.

'Thank you, Nurse, for agreeing to come with Wendy and me,' he said, for all the world as if she had had any say in the arrangement.

'Before she joins us, sir, may I know what her trouble is, please?'

He glanced at the house briefly, than back at Bryony. 'She has kidney trouble after living in Saudi Arabia. The very dry climate made her become dehydrated and she has had stones so we are on the look-out for renal colic or if she should pass blood.'

Bryony nodded sympathetically. 'Poor little girl, that is very painful. Is she your only child?'

He looked surprised. 'Wendy is my godchild, the daughter of a colleague. Her parents brought her home when she became ill and it was decided that she should live with my mother and myself. Unfortunately Mother has had to go to California for a time so Wendy is alone with my housekeeper and me.'

'So that is why she looked so sad and lonely,' Bryony said, remembering.

'Thank you very much, Nurse.' He wrinkled up his forehead and turned down the corners of his mouth.

The colour flooded her cheeks. Couldn't she ever say anything right to this man?

'I'm sorry—I didn't mean—'

He looked down at her with laughing eyes. 'You are quite right, of course. That is why I have taken time off to show her a little of Cornwall and give her the benefit of your company which I am quite sure will be a vast improvement.'

She tensed her muscles, hating him. Before she could think of a reply, which was just as well, the little girl walked slowly down the steps from the house. Her heavy, dark-ringed eyes were fixed on Bryony. She was painfully thin and Bryony had a sudden fierce longing to take her in her arms and cuddle her.

She held out a friendly hand. 'Hello Wendy, isn't it fun that Dr Crosland is taking us out for the day? I'm looking forward to it, aren't you?'

She slipped her hand in Bryony's. 'You mean Uncle Ellis?'

'This is Nurse Sellers, Wendy, who has kindly agreed to come with us,' said Dr Crosland.

'Hello Nurse Sellers,' she said politely. Then turned to ask, 'Where are you going to take us?'

'Well now, let me look at the map.' He took it from the dashboard of his Porsche and studied it as he leaned against the light grey car. 'Yes. We will go to Madron and from there to Zennor and St Ives. Then we will see what the time is and how we feel. In the car, ladies.'

As Bryony was about to get into the back seat Dr Crosland placed a detaining hand on her arm.

'The back seats in this car are not very comfortable for two, it would be better for you to sit in the front.'

He drove swiftly up the hill which led away from the sea front and through Heamoor. When they had gone past Madron he parked the car at the side of the road.

'There is a baptistery and a wishing well nearby which you might like to see, but we will have to walk the rest of the way.'

Wendy scrambled out of the car. 'A wishing well, Uncle Ellis? Can I have a wish?'

'You could if you had a pin, Wendy.'

She felt in the pockets of her dress. Then she shook her head.

'I haven't got one, Uncle Ellis. Why have I got to have one?'

Bryony opened her handbag. 'Here we are. No nurse is complete without a pin.'

They climbed over a stile and walked along a footpath through several fields until they came to a sign-post which pointed to the wishing well.

'It's here, it's really here!' Wendy cried excitedly.

'Once upon a time on a May morning the village girls always came here to make a wish,' Dr Crosland said.

'And did they come true? Will mine?'

He raised his eyebrows. 'Who knows?'

'I'm sure it will, Wendy,' Bryony said.

They came to a narrow cinder path overgrown with nettles. The doctor lifted Wendy easily with one arm.

'You don't want to sting your legs. How about you, Nurse? I have another free arm.' He looked at her with sparkling yellow eyes.

She shook her head. The mere thought of such a thing sent the blood coursing through her cheeks.

He took the pin from Wendy and bent it. 'There you are. Throw it over your shoulder and wish at the same time. But you mustn't tell anyone what you wished or it won't come true.'

Wendy threw the pin so determinedly that she almost toppled over backwards.

'There, that has settled your future happiness satisfactorily,' Dr Crosland said, hugging Wendy to his side.

They retraced their steps to the sign-post and walked a short way in the other direction to see the baptistery ruins where only the walls and the remains of stone seats and the altar slab were standing, after the assault on it by the Puritans in the seventeenth century.

'Somewhere here is a holy well which is said to be almost as famous for cures as Lourdes, but I'm afraid I don't know where it is.'

'Do you believe it would work?' Bryony asked.

He gave her a sideways smile and her heart leapt in her breast.

'I wouldn't like to swear that it wouldn't, so I'm keeping quiet about it. If more people knew of it I'd be doing myself out of a job.'

They got back into the car and drove on through lanes bordered by massive bushes of rhododendrons in every shade of red and pink and purple. They came out on to the beautiful north coast road which ran through rugged moorland which was a blaze of colour with yellow gorse and stretches of purple heather surrounded by ferns and bracken and brambles. On the northern side cliffs hung down in great rocky slabs to the deep blue sea which tossed up fountains of spray.

Beautiful though the scenery was, Bryony's eyes constantly strayed to the man at her side. To the long-fingered hands that lay lightly on the steering-wheel, to the length of expensive trouser leg, to the tanned neck in the open-necked shirt, the strong nose and mouth, the yellow eyes and the finely-etched lines that radiated from them, and the hair that shone like a new chestnut.

'We are coming to Zennor,' he told them as they reached the top of a very steep hill. 'There is a museum here which holds old mining and farm equipment. Would you like a quick look around?'

When they had done so they walked on to the church which was at the top of a flight of moss-covered steps. On the tower wall was a bronze sundial inscribed with the words, 'The glory of the world passeth', engraved on it was the figure of a mermaid.

'That is the mermaid of Zennor,' Ellis said.

Wendy tugged at his hand. 'A mermaid, Uncle Ellis? Tell me. Tell me about her. Was she a really real mermaid?'

He smiled down at her and gently brushed aside the hair which had fallen across her face.

'So they say, Wendy. It is the legend of a squire's son who sang so sweetly in the church choir that a mermaid who lived in the cove down below heard him and fell in love with him. She attended the services and at last lured him to her home under the sea and he was never heard of again.'

Wendy stared up at him and chewed her bottom lip. 'I don't think I like that story very much.'

'No? Well how do you like this one. Many years ago, villagers had to pay the church a tithe, or a tenth of what money they earned from their cows and calves. But on one occasion four villagers brought in to the church butter and cheese instead of money and the parson ordered them to be removed for they were "an indecency and a nuisance".'

'I don't like it either,' Wendy said, playing with a button on his jacket.

Ellis looked at Bryony and smiled. 'I don't seem to be doing too well. Where have I gone wrong, Nurse?'

She laughed. 'Wendy probably prefers reading Enid Blyton to fairy stories, like lots of children nowadays.'

'Fairy stories, Nurse?' he said, pretending indignation. 'What I have told her are genuine Cornish legends, things she should know. Well, shall we carry on to St Ives?'

As they neared the town Ellis drove slowly. 'There is a good hotel here. Would you like lunch now or would you prefer to spend some time looking round first? It is quite early.'

Bryony turned to Wendy. 'What do you say, Wendy? Are you hungry?'

She shook her head. 'No, I want to go down to the sea.'

When they had parked the car they made their way down the steep, narrow streets that led to the fishing harbour and the lovely beach. On their way they passed the studio where Barbara Hepworth, the sculptress, had lived and worked, but which was now a museum where paintings by local artists were displayed.

'St Ives is second only to London in importance in the world of art,' Ellis said. 'There are numerous potters here too—there are in many parts of Cornwall—and very excellent work they do.'

They had a quick look inside the church of St Ia so that Wendy and Bryony could see the engraved front panels of the choir stalls which showed a man and woman in period dress and a blacksmith's tools, and admire the carvings on the wagon roof.

Everywhere was bright with holiday-makers who thronged the roads and the beach. With the many-coloured sailing boats and the quaint cottages with unexpected palm trees in their front gardens it looked very picturesque, like some Mediterranean town.

The sun was warm as they leaned on the railings which edged the harbour.

Wendy tugged Bryony's arm.

'Yes dear?' she asked anxiously.

'Don't they look nice,' she said softly.

Bryony looked around her to see what she was referring to. A family sitting nearby on the harbour wall were eating steaming hot Cornish pasties.

'Don't what look nice, Wendy?'

'Those—those pies.' She looked at them longingly.

Bryony scarcely knew what to do. She remembered when she was a child how good something would taste if it was something out of the ordinary.

A piece of bacon from her father's plate, a bun or biscuit fresh from the oven, or some of the sugar in candied peel when her mother was chopping it for Christmas cakes and puddings. She had to admit that the pasties were mouth-watering with their oniony smell. But on this occasion they 'had better love a dream'. Lunch was to be taken at the hotel on the hill. Ellis had said so.

'Yes, they do look good, Wendy,' she said.

She was turning away when she suddenly thought, why shouldn't Wendy have a pasty if that was what she fancied? Dr Crosland could go to the hotel by himself.

'Dr Crosland,' she said, her voice croaking. She was annoyed to feel her heart beating fast.

'Yes Nurse?' He looked apprehensively from her to Wendy as if he feared something might be amiss.

'I—I wonder . . .' she began. Then, moistening her lips she started again. 'Wendy and I would like to have a pasty and eat it here on the beach. Would you mind? We could meet up with you later.'

She knew that she was being discourteous and she dreaded to think of what Sister Mailer would have said if she had heard her, but she felt this was an opportunity to give Wendy pleasure which should not be missed.

He looked at her unsmilingly and then at Wendy. 'Would you prefer that to going to the hotel for a proper lunch?'

Wendy's face brightened. 'Oh, yes please,

Uncle, I would prefer it a lot much more.'

'And you, Nurse?'

Bryony smiled down at Wendy. 'Yes, I would like that too. But please—I will get them. You carry on to the hotel.'

He shook his head. 'Find yourselves a spot on the beach and I will bring them to you.'

When he returned with three hot pasties Bryony felt embarrassed. She had forgotten the need to treat him as a demi-god. Moreover, it *would* have been nicer to sit at a table in a comfortable hotel and have a good meal, for these pasties were decidedly stodgy and filled mostly with potato. She glanced at him from under her lashes. He looked all wrong sitting on the sand in his expensive clothes, surrounded by bathers and children making sand castles. She should have thought of that before she made the suggestion but it was not in her nature to do so. Then she saw that Wendy looked supremely happy. There were pastry crumbs and pieces of potato on her dress and her hair was blowing all over the place, but the bleak look on her face which had so worried Bryony had disappeared. And she had eaten her pasty all up.

'Did you enjoy that?' Bryony asked.

Wendy nodded contentedly. 'It was smashing.'

'Would you like to have an ice-cream now?'

'Yes please.' She gave a rare smile.

Bryony scrambled to her feet. 'I'd like to get Wendy an ice, if that's all right? May she have one?'

'Sure.' He pushed himself up off the beach. 'You stay here with Wendy. I'll go.'

He returned with three large cornets. 'I can't remember the last one of these I had. I feel I've been missing something,' he said.

She felt sorry for him. There were so many ordinary things that a person of his eminence could not do. He certainly could not walk along the esplanade at Polwithy licking an ice-cream or eating fish and chips.

'I think that Wendy and I would like to freshen up. The ice-cream has made us sticky. So shall we meet you here? Come along Wendy.'

When they had washed their hands Bryony combed Wendy's hair. 'Do you feel uncomfortable with it blowing about your face? Would you rather have it tied up in a pony-tail?'

'What's a pony-tail?' Wendy's tired eyes stared up at her.

'You tie a piece of ribbon round it like this and it keeps the hair off your face,' Bryony explained.

'I think that sounds a good idea. Only I haven't got any ribbon.'

'What's your favourite colour?'

Wendy put her head on one side and chewed her lips thoughtfully. 'Blue. Bright blue.'

'Okay, we'll see whether we can buy some blue ribbon.'

They chose a pretty blue satin and Bryony tied Wendy's hair with it right away. 'How do you like that?' Bryony held up her small mirror.

Wendy gave a wide smile, and tossed the clump of hair to and fro. 'It's lovely,' she said and slipped her hand in Bryony's.

When they neared Ellis, Wendy ran up to him excitedly. 'Look at me, look at me, Uncle Ellis. Look at my hair.'

Only then did Bryony realise that she had overstepped her role as accompanying nurse.

'I—I hope you don't mind,' she faltered. 'But her hair was all over her face and . . .'

He looked at her thoughtfully for a moment, then turned to Wendy.

'You look very smart. Did you thank Nurse?'

It was so pleasant on the beach that they decided to stay there for the rest of the afternoon. Despite Bryony's fears and doubts she had thoroughly enjoyed the outing and hoped that the others had as well. She felt sure that Wendy had, but Dr Crosland wore a pensive look at times. She believed that his thoughts were on his patients and he was debating with himself about the treatment he had prescribed. She knew that he was paid handsomely for his work but nevertheless she had never seen a doctor who gave out so much compassion, empathy, knowledge and time as he appeared to, nor one who showed so much concern for his patients' welfare. She gave a sigh of contentment, feeling privileged to have been invited to spend a day in his company.

They were passing Polwithy hospital as they neared home, and a young, smartly-dressed woman with brilliant copper-coloured hair whom Bryony recognised as Dr Thea Browne, the hospital's medical registrar, was about to go through the gates.

Dr Crosland gave a short blast on his car horn to attract her attention. She gave a delighted smile and came across.

'Hello Ellis,' she began, then suddenly stopped as she saw Bryony and Wendy. 'Hi, Wendy, where have you been?' she asked uninterestedly.

Wendy tossed her head self-consciously. 'To St Ives to buy my hair ribbon,' she said proudly.

'I decided it was time for Wendy to see something of Cornwall and Nurse kindly agreed to accompany her. Do you know one another? Nurse Sellers—Dr Browne.'

Thea's round brown eyes wandered coldly over Bryony. 'Oh, a nurse from Highfields, I suppose. How do you do.' She turned swiftly away to speak to Ellis again.

'Don't forget tomorrow night at my place. Eight o'clock.'

'I hadn't forgotten,' he said. He gave a slight wave, then drove on.

For Bryony the pleasure of the day had disappeared like Cornish mist in sunshine. After all she was just a nurse who had accompanied a sick child. She had no one to blame but herself for pretending for a short time that they were a man, a woman and a child on a picnic, enjoying themselves like friends—or more.

CHAPTER FOUR

NURSE Dyson was writing up her case notes—'Complains of pain in legs' she had written on Mrs Chamberlain's chart and was about to add another line when Bryony arrived on duty.

'How are your knees?' she asked chirpily.

'My knees?' Bryony glanced down at them. 'They're okay. Shouldn't they be?'

Rene grinned. 'Not with all that bowing and scraping you had to do yesterday.'

Bryony flushed. 'It wasn't like that. He—he was very amiable. I went along to keep an eye on Wendy, his god-daughter, that's all.'

'So why pick on you? A newcomer?' There was a note of envy in her voice.

Bryony was alarmed. The last thing she wanted was to alienate Rene Dyson, her only friend in Highfields.

'I asked Sister that,' she said hastily. 'And she told me in no uncertain terms that you would have been far more suitable but that I was expendable and you were not!'

Rene appeared satisfied. 'So where did you go?'

'To St Ives, around Zennor.' She was about to tell of their pasty lunch but managed to stop herself in time. To have mentioned it would have meant that the incident would be relayed all over the nursing home and she certainly did not want it to reach Dr Crosland's ears.

'Is that all?'

'Yes. Wendy enjoyed it I think. She leads a very lonely life.'

'Poor kid. I heard she has kidney trouble. She couldn't be in better hands, could she?'

'Did anything of moment happen in my absence?' Bryony asked.

'Yes, a young woman was admitted with a suspected ulcer. She's due to go for X-ray now. Will you take her? She's in room six.'

'Right. I'm on my way.'

The patient was a married woman aged twenty-four. She was painfully thin and wore an anxious look on her face. She looked up nervously when Bryony entered the room.

Bryony glanced at her notes and saw that she had a history of continuing indigestion with severe pain and vomiting.

'Mrs Boase. Is that right?'

'Yes. Rosemary Boase.'

'And you were admitted yesterday. What led up to that?'

'I had to do something, I've felt so dreadful for years and all my own doctor would say was that I had nervous indigestion and the medicine and tablets he gave me never did any good at all. My husband heard how excellent Dr Crosland was and he said that I should see him. So I did and Dr Crosland said I must come in here for tests.'

Her inexpensive dressing-gown and slippers showed Bryony that by comparison with the other patients she was hard-up and she hoped that her stay would not be longer than necessary.

'Righto. We'll go along to X-ray.'

On their way there a patient's door opened and Dr Crosland and Sister Mailer came out. Bryony's heart leapt but she looked fixedly at the floor so as not to be found guilty of undue familiarity.

'Good morning Mrs Boase. You are off for your X-ray?' he asked pleasantly.

Bryony could not resist peeping at him from under her eyelashes. His eyes were warm and compassionate. He is magnetic, she thought, no other word will do.

'Yes Doctor,' Mrs Boase said breathlessly.

'Splendid.' He nodded and smiled and walked on.

When he was out of earshot Mrs Boase said with a sigh,

'Isn't he gorgeous! When I first saw how young and handsome he was I felt terribly embarrassed at having to undress for him to examine me. But he seemed to know just how I felt and somehow it was all right.'

'He is a doctor and so far as he is concerned seeing a woman undressed is a daily occurrence,' Bryony said matter-of-factly.

'How lucky you are to work with him! He's got

everything, looks, manners, voice, clothes, brains—'

'And money,' Bryony said acidly, irritated at hearing yet another person extolling his virtues.

'Yes, and money. Brian, that's my husband, couldn't really afford to pay his fee but he got fed up with me feeling ill all the time so we managed to scrape the money together. And I'm glad because I feel sure he will be able to do something for me.'

'I hope so. Having faith in him is a big step in the right direction.'

Bryony sat in the corridor and waited while the pictures were taken. It was very different from St Stephen's where there were queues of people waiting and it could take the whole morning. Here Mrs Boase was in and out in a few minutes.

'I'm sure you would like something to eat now, as you couldn't have any breakfast. What can I get you?'

Mrs Boase sighed. 'Whatever I have it is sure to upset me. But I would like some coffee, please.'

'You should try and eat something. Would you like a boiled egg and some thin bread and butter?'

'Only if the egg is very lightly boiled. I find that coddled is best.' She looked anxiously at Bryony. 'I don't want to be any trouble, I know it isn't mealtime.'

Bryony smiled at her. 'You are no trouble, Mrs Boase, we want you to be comfortable. All you have to do is ask, and like fairy godmothers we give it to you if we can.'

When she had seen that Mrs Boase was comfortably settled with her meal Bryony went on to Winston Deansborough's room. In contrast to Rosemary Boase, all his possessions were ornate and expensive. On the dressing-table his ivory-backed brushes had his initials on them in gold. Bottles and bowls in crystal had gold tops. His turquoise pyjamas were made of pure silk and slung around his shoulders was a matching robe. The sunlight sent a myriad of lights from the diamonds on his fingers.

'Good morning Mr Deansborough, I hope you are feeling better. I'll just take your temperature if I may.'

She placed the thermometer under his tongue and held his wrist between her thumb and forefinger.

'That's fine. No problems there at all. Now I'd like to see what your blood pressure is doing.'

She wrapped the cuff of the sphygmomanometer around his arm and tightened it.

'That's fine too. Have you any idea when Dr Crosland will discharge you?'

He smiled and showed a row of very white teeth. 'You make me sound like a gun, Nurse.'

She laughed, realising that the jargon used in St Stephen's was not necessarily the same as here.

'When do you expect to leave, Mr Deansborough?'

'I do not wish to leave until I am quite recovered. I have no intention of going from here with an elbow crutch. I will either walk from here like a well man or stay here for ever.'

'Well my bet is that you'll soon be doing the former.'

'Your Dr Crosland is a very clever man. He knew what my trouble was, no problem. Very different from other doctors I have consulted. He is a good man.'

'I see,' Bryony joked, 'you like him so much you don't want to leave?'

The smile left Winston's face. 'I respect him very much. I will not leave here until he says "Winston, you may go". When he does that, I will know that I am very fine.'

Mrs Trengwainton was the next patient on Bryony's list. She raised her hand in greeting.

'Ah, here you are, Nurse. I missed you yesterday.'

'It's good to be missed,' Bryony smiled. 'How are you feeling?' She reached for the thermometer.

Her eyes travelled over Bryony from her fair hair to her dainty toes, then back to her oval face.

'Bored, Nurse. I am beginning to feel I should like to be home.'

'Your temperature and pulse rate are satisfactory, have you spoken to Dr Crosland about leaving?'

'Leaving!' Her pale eyes looked shocked. 'I couldn't possibly leave. There are only the servants at home and nobody to look after me.'

Once again Bryony wondered why she was being kept there in Highfields. Nothing was being done for her and nothing apparently needed to be done. If it was just a holiday that she fancied she would be better off in a hotel, it would be more wholesome than imagining herself to be an invalid. She would have had her marching orders long since at St Stephen's. But there, of course, she would not have been lining Dr Crosland's pockets.

'It's a very nice morning, do you fancy sitting in the garden?'

'Yes, I think I would enjoy that for a while, but don't leave me there indefinitely.'

'As if I would, Mrs Trengwainton. I will see that you come in when you feel like it.'

When she had settled her high up on the lawn where she could get a good view of the sea, arranged cushions in the small of her back and a footstool, placed a table by her side with two reading books, her glasses, a box of chocolates and a bell to summon assistance, Bryony returned to her other patients.

She gave a blanket bath to an eighty-one year old man who said he had no intention of climbing into a bath, it was asking for trouble and he had enough of that to contend with.

'You could easily hop into that bath if you had a mind to,' Bryony said teasingly. 'It's my opinion you are just plain lazy.'

He closed a wicked, rheumy eye. 'That isn't the

reason, Nurse. But I'm not going to turn down the chance of a pretty little thing like you bathing me. I'm not too old to enjoy that.'

'Really, Mr Godstone, I am surprised at you,' Bryony said in mock rebuke. But his remark had not affected her at all. At St Stephen's nurses frequently had far more salacious remarks made to them and took them in their stride.

When she eventually went to the dining-room Nurse Dyson was already there. Bryony got her coffee and joined her.

'I can't stop long, Mrs Trengwainton is sitting in the garden and I promised to keep an eye on her.'

'Oh she'd have us all running. She's been spoilt all her life if you ask me.'

Bryony nibbled a biscuit thoughtfully. 'Do you think there is anything the matter with her?'

'No, I shouldn't think so.'

'Then why do you imagine she is here?'

'Ours is not to reason why. She'll be here as long as Dr Crosland thinks necessary.'

'It's as well she has the money to pay. I do hope he doesn't keep the Boase woman in long.'

'Why? What have you got against her?'

'Nothing at all, she's rather sweet. But she can't really afford to stay here, she told me her husband had to scrape the money together to pay the consultation fee and didn't think that she was going to be admitted.'

'Well it would be a wasted effort if she left before

Dr Crosland had the chance to do something for her.'

'I suppose so.'

'Oh, in case you don't know, Polwithy General is holding their annual dance on Saturday, it's to boost their finances. We who are off duty are expected to attend. Our lord and master demands it.'

Bryony frowned. 'I wish you hadn't told me, then I could have pleaded ignorance. I don't want to go, and I can't go without a partner, I wouldn't know anyone there.'

'You'll know me, I'm going and I'll enjoy it.'

'Are you going alone?'

Rene smiled self-consciously. 'Strange though it may seem I have an admirer who will come along to keep me from the groping hands of the dishy doctors, ha, ha!'

'It doesn't seem strange at all. Who is this lucky man?'

'Need you ask? He owns a cake shop in the town, that's why I picked on him,' she grinned.

'Heavens! If he marries you the poor bloke will go bankrupt.' Bryony laughed. 'But seriously, you don't imagine that I'm going to play gooseberry, do you?'

'No, it won't be like that at all. I get puffed dancing and Ken loves it so I'll be only too glad for you to take my place occasionally. But if you pinch him off me I'll have your guts for garters,' she threatened.

'Oh very nicely put, that is what I consider real Highfields talk,' Bryony said, pretending disapproval.

When the night of the dance came, Bryony found she was quite looking forward to it, it was so long since she had had a night out—not since her broken engagement. She wore her favourite dress, an off-the-shoulder peach silk. She used matching blusher on her cheeks and a deeper shade of lipstick. She had naturally dark eyelashes but nevertheless brushed them with mascara. Her ear-rings were tiny wisps of gold and matched her necklace.

She went rather reluctantly into the hall for she scarcely knew any of the people there, she had not been at Polwithy long enough to have met many of the hospital staff. With a feeling of relief she saw that Rene was already there and bounding around the floor with a jolly-looking young man, both of them apparently in the best of spirits. Dr Thea Browne's brilliant auburn hair and slinky green dress made her immediately noticeable even in that crowded hall. Bryony's eyes searched the knot of men around her and her breath caught in her throat. Ellis Crosland was one of them and looked both immaculate and very handsome, head and shoulders above the others, in Bryony's opinion. She watched enviously as he laid his hand possessively on Thea's waist, then led her into the dance. She was oblivious to everything and everybody else. Only when a man who was standing just behind her spoke, did she even know that he was there.

'They make a very striking looking couple, don't they?'

Bryony turned and gave him a fleeting glance. 'Who?' she asked foolishly.

'Our own Thea and Dr Crosland. Don't you know them? She is the lovely auburn-haired girl. Lucky Dr Crosland, I say. Shall we dance?'

Bryony realised that nobody could have been a more uninteresting, dull partner for this poor young man than herself. She gave brief noncommittal replies to his light-hearted conversation, scarcely knowing what he said.

It was with a look of intense relief that he suddenly released her and she realised that it was an Excuse Me dance. She gave him an apologetic smile and turned to look up at her saviour. Then she began to tremble as Dr Crosland's arm encircled her, seeming to scorch her body through the thin material of her dress. He held her close and she knew that he must be aware of the thudding, uneven beat of her heart.

After a few minutes he held her away from him. She looked up, afraid that someone had tapped him on the shoulder and that he was going to leave her. But her fear was unfounded. His dark honey-coloured eyes were warm with admiration.

'You are looking very attractive, Nurse. That's a pretty frock.'

She laughed. 'That's a funny word to use.'

'What? Attractive?'

'No. Frock. It's a dress.'

'Oh?' He raised his eyebrows. 'Now I wonder what the difference is.'

She shook her head, her fair hair swinging from side to side. 'All right, it's a frock! I'm very surprised to see so many people here. Polwithy General must be much bigger than I realised.'

He looked at her in surprise. 'Oh, haven't you been over the hospital yet?'

'No. I haven't had any reason to go there.'

His eyes searched the hall. 'We must rectify that. I'll have a word with Dr Browne and perhaps she will arrange to show you around.'

Bryony felt a pang of dismay. She could not imagine anything she would like less than to be escorted by the unfriendly Dr Browne.

'Oh please don't bother,' she said hastily. 'Apart from size I don't suppose it is any different from St Stephen's.'

As soon as she had spoken, the words seemed to float on the air and she realised how rude she must have sounded.

'Oh, I am sorry. I didn't mean—what I meant was—' Her sentence trailed away.

She glanced up at him to see if he was offended and surprised a flicker in his eyes which could have been amusement, but that was impossible.

After a moment of uncomfortable silence, he said, 'By the way, you made a big hit with Wendy.'

Bryony smiled with pleasure. 'I am so glad. She is a dear little girl and I enjoyed being with her.'

And with you, she added silently. I enjoyed that more than I could ever say.

'Good. Then we must arrange another outing for her. She is a lonely child, she knows nobody. It will be much better when she starts school.'

'When will that be?'

'Provided that she continues to make good progress, health-wise, she will start in September, when the new school year begins.'

The music stopped and Bryony glanced towards the band reproachfully. Dr Crosland smiled and thanked her, then led her to a chair.

'You are with friends?'

'Yes,' she replied.

'Then, if you'll excuse me?'

He went to join a group of doctors. He made some remark and there was a burst of laughter. She had a sick feeling in her stomach. He was so jolly and friendly with them and she wanted desperately to be one of them.

Rene and her partner saw Bryony and came across to her. Rene flopped on to the chair beside her.

'Hello, love. Here we are, Bryony, this is Ken. My two best friends. I saw you leaning lovingly against the manly bosom of—' she bobbed a curtsey, 'the one and only Dr Crosland. So who's hob-nobbing with the hierarchy?'

Bryony laughed to cover her embarrassment.

'This girl talks a lot of rubbish, haven't you noticed?'

Ken nodded. 'So what shall we do about her?'

Bryony studied her with her head on one side. 'Feed her?' she suggested.

'Okay. You two sit here and I'll fetch you something.'

'You'll need a trolley to bring enough to satisfy Rene!'

When he had gone Rene mopped her streaming forehead with her handkerchief.

'I love these dances when we all get together. Not literally, of course, for it's very much a case of "them" and "us". But at least we can see how the other half disports itself.'

'How do you mean?'

'Why, doctors v nursing staff of course. That barrier may be invisible, but oh boy, it's there all right!'

'If you feel like that, why do you enjoy it?'

'Because I've got a lot of friends here and the others give it a bit of class. But I don't want to be one of "them", the snobbery amongst them is unbelievable. Status counts for more in the medical profession than anywhere else, I should think. Silly, isn't it? I can't stand that sort of thing. I'm surprised at myself for staying at Highfields.' She looked across the room. 'Isn't Dr Browne looking smashing? She's a very attractive woman and clever with it. Yet what is her aim in life?'

Bryony shook her head. 'I haven't a clue.'

'Why, it's to be Mrs Ellis Crosland, of course, God help her. A consultant who is the owner of Highfields and a medical registrar in one family is going to keep them off the bread-line, don't you reckon?'

With every word the good-hearted Rene spoke, Bryony's spirits sank lower and lower. She was almost counting the minutes before she could reasonably say it was time for her to leave.

At long last she was able to do so. As she was on her way to collect her coat she felt a hand on her arm, and by the thrill which caused her to jump, she knew without looking that it was Ellis Crosland.

'Nurse Sellers, I have had a word with Dr Browne and she has agreed to take my clinic on Thursday, so that I shall be free to take Wendy out. I should like you to accompany us if you will.'

He raised an eyebrow but did not wait or seem to expect a reply. 'I will have a word with Sister Mailer and make it all right.'

'Thank you,' Bryony murmured.

Then he was gone, striding around the perimeter of the hall to rejoin Dr Browne.

CHAPTER FIVE

'Dr Crosland has seen my X-rays and he says that I have definitely got an ulcer. It's only very tiny, apparently, and doesn't show up well on the X-ray. But he can see it and he says that the small ones can cause more pain sometimes than the big ones,' Rosemary Boase told Bryony.

'Is it a duodenal?'

'Yes, that's right.'

'Well now that the trouble has been located Dr Crosland will be able to treat it.'

The girl gave a long, contented sigh.

'What's that for?' Bryony asked in surprise.

'I'm so glad he found one. I've been so fed up with being told over and over again that I've got nervous indigestion when I was positive it was something more than that. I would have put up with being told it was something dreadful, I think. I never want to hear the words "nervous indigestion" again.' She gave a rueful smile.

'Well fortunately it wasn't something dreadful, and with any luck you should soon feel a whole lot better.'

The patient with hepatitis was being moved to the surgical wing after an X-ray and tests showed that the blockage of her bile duct was caused by stones and not catarrh.

Winston Deansborough was sitting up in bed with a scowl on his handsome face.

Bryony put up her hands and pretended to back away from him. 'My goodness, look out that the wind doesn't change or you may get stuck like that.'

'What wind is that? What does "stuck like that" mean, please?' he asked sulkily.

'Forget it Mr Deansborough. I was wondering why you were looking so angry.'

'Because I *am* angry. Dr Crosland has given me an elbow crutch and says it is to help me walk, but I cannot do that.'

'You can't? Why is that?'

'Because I am used to walking with two legs and not one silly arm on a crutch to help me along.'

'I know it isn't easy at first but you'll be surprised how quickly you will get used to it. Will you try? Just to please me?' She looked at him with her head on one side and smiled encouragingly. 'Let me see you try.'

His eyes were as black as coal and his lips firmly compressed as he made the effort. After a while Bryony said,

'That's right, you're getting better all the time. Now will you promise me to practise using it for ten minutes?'

He gave a ferocious scowl as she left the room, and she hurried along the corridor to visit Mrs Trengwainton. Here she was welcomed effusively.

'Oh good, I've been hoping you would come today. I have had a wonderful idea. I am beginning to feel that I can see the light at the end of the tunnel.'

'Oh yes? That's good,' Bryony said, wondering what she meant.

'I can visualize that the time will come when I can return home.'

Bryony smiled at her warmly. 'Splendid, I'm so glad. I do feel that you will quickly get stronger in your own home. What does Dr Crosland say?'

'Oh I haven't told him and I won't until I get your answer.'

'My answer to what?'

'Sit down Nurse. Bring over that comfortable chair because I want to talk to you.'

Bryony thought of the many things she had to do but knew that in Highfields pleasing Mrs Trengwainton had to come high on the list of priorities.

'Yes, Mrs Trengwainton?'

'Now, Nurse, as you know, I am not at all well and I need to have someone with medical knowledge within call. I live just outside Falmouth in a large house which overlooks the Helford river, a lovely area. I have several girls working under my housekeeper and a man and a boy who do my garden. People come from all over the country to see it, they keep it very nicely. However, they all look after the house and grounds. I want someone pleasant to look after me personally. And I think that you would be most suitable. What do you think of that?' She looked at Bryony like a school governor bestowing on a head girl a special prize for excellence during the school year.

Bryony was appalled. 'But Mrs Trengwainton, I—'

She held up an imperious, restraining hand. 'Wait, please, and allow me to continue. You have not been here long so I am sure there would be no difficulty in getting Dr Crosland to release you from whatever contract or arrangement you have entered into. You may be wondering why I have chosen you and I will tell you right away that it is because I feel you would suit my household well and be acceptable to my many friends. You speak well, you have a pleasant manner and you look attractive. I can't bear plump girls who perspire. So what do you say?'

Bryony stared at her with glazed eyes. 'I—I am very flattered, Mrs Trengwainton, and it is very kind of you, but I—'

'Allow me to continue, please. I don't know what they pay you here but I am willing to double it. You will of course have your own rooms, bathroom etcetera, and we would not quarrel over anything you needed. Do you drive?'

Bryony said hesitantly, 'I have a licence but I haven't done—'

'Splendid. Then we will get you a little car for your own use. You know how easy I am to get along with so there would be no problem there. What notice will you have to give?'

Bryony was thankful that she was sitting down for she feared that her legs would not support her. Mrs Trengwainton was offering her so much, surely any person in her right mind would be overjoyed. But although she had only been at Highfields for a short time it had been long enough for her to have become attached to it and to Rene and Sister Mailer and most of the patients. She wondered who she thought she was fooling. She knew that the one person who could keep her here, even though she knew it was foolish to feel that way, was Dr Crosland. The thought of day following day and week following week without the chance of seeing him, even if it were merely passing him in the corridor when she couldn't speak to him, made her feel that the rest of her life would be like a long dreary road which led to nowhere.

She glanced at Mrs Trengwainton's tired, bored eyes, which nevertheless today had a hopeful look in them and realised that she was a lonely, even frightened woman despite all her wordly wealth. So although she wanted to refuse her offer she felt unable immediately and irrevocably to dash her hopes. She looked down at the satin bedspread and said awkwardly,

'It sounds a marvellous offer, but it has come as such a surprise I—I would like to think it over. I'm sure you understand.' She gave her a sweet, shy smile.

'Well of course I do. Take your time, I am in no great hurry to leave here. But I think you would be happy with me, and I with you.'

'Thank you, Mrs Trengwainton, I will let you know when I have made up my mind. And now, is there anything I can do for you?'

When she had adjusted the curtains a little to shield her from the sun, Bryony left and went to the dining-room. She poured herself some coffee from the jug which stood on the counter, helped herself to hot milk and carried her cup over to a table by the window, looking out over the kitchen garden and the orchard where the trees were laden with small green apples which gave promise of a good harvest later in the year. It was such a different scene from the traffic-filled streets and high-rise office blocks which formed the outlook from St Stephen's canteen. This was so beautiful, just what she had wanted when she sought a new beginning. To leave now, to make another change would surely be unwise. Moreover, life with Mrs Trengwainton would give her too much solitude and time in which to remember Nick and what might have been. But it was a tempting offer, the chance of a lifetime. She had been promised that within reason she could ask for anything she wanted. But what she wanted most in the world it was not in Mrs Trengwainton's power to give. She could not give her Dr Crosland, could she?

The rows of green vegetables and fruit bushes blurred and Bryony did not see them. She was picturing a tall, lithe man, with a lock of chestnut hair on his forehead, a firm shapely mouth and eyes like topaz, that were sometimes cool and impersonal and at other times warm and deeply compassionate. Even thinking about him gave her a thrill of sensuous pleasure and she wondered just what it was about him that made him so irresistible.

On her way back on duty she met Rene hurrying along the corridor.

'Ha, ha! I beat you to it. I've had my coffee,' Bryony said cheerfully.

'Mrs Andrewartha's pleurisy has taken a turn for the worse. Dr Crosland is with her,' Rene whispered hurriedly and disappeared into room number five.

Bryony continued along the corridor to Winston's room. Beads of perspiration stood on his forehead and there was a drained look on his face.

'What's the matter? What has happened?' Bryony asked anxiously.

'Ever since you left me I have been walking up and down, up and down. Soon I will walk without this crutch and then I will go home like a man,' he said triumphantly.

'Well I don't think it's a good idea to overdo the exercise at first,' Bryony said, annoyed with herself for not returning sooner.

'Why? Why is it not good to do that?' he demanded, the triumph fading from his face.

'Oh—you'll wear out our carpet,' she said lightly.

He smiled again, showing his excellent teeth. 'You joke with me! I thought I had done myself wrong to walk so much and I should not like to do that. Dr Crosland has been so good I must not spoil for him his cure.'

'I don't think you will have done that,' Bryony said reassuringly.

With Mrs Trengwainton talking about leaving and now Winston having the same idea Bryony wondered with a secret wry smile how Dr Crosland was going to like having his income curtailed. She could not understand herself. Feeling as she did about him, why did she nevertheless begrudge him the money he earned? But in the recesses of her mind she *did* know, it was because of the bitter lesson that Nick had taught her.

She was busily sorting linen when an auxiliary found her and told her that she was wanted in Sister Mailer's office. With her mind still on Mrs Trengwainton's tempting offer she did not, as she would normally have done, wonder why she had been summoned there. She tapped on the door and was told to enter.

She felt the colour flood her cheeks when she saw that Dr Crosland was also in the room.

'You sent for me, Sister?'

'Indeed I did, Nurse Sellers. Dr Crosland has something to say to you.' Her face was unsmiling.

Bryony looked up at him questioningly. Never before had she seen his lips so compressed, his nostrils so flared, his eyes so hostile, and she was afraid.

He said with a snap and a blaze of annoyance, 'I

have just seen Mr Deansborough and he is completely exhausted. It seems that you told him to practise walking with his elbow crutch. Is that so?'

Bryony's eyes widened. 'Why yes, sir. I—'

'And you went away and left him for over an hour?'

'Yes, but I—'

He cut her short and said irritably, 'Do you realise that such negligence has set him back for at least a week, possibly longer?'

Bryony felt the shame of a rush of tears to her eyes. She tensed her muscles. In no way was she going to allow them to fall. Unblinking, she said through stiff lips,

'I am sorry, sir, but I did tell him to try and walk for only ten minutes.'

'Then you should have stayed with him for that time. Where were you?' he demanded.

'In—in Mrs Trengwainton's room and—and then I went for coffee,' she faltered.

He raised his arm ostentatiously and looked at his wrist-watch.

'For coffee?' he exploded.

She made no reply, just stared fixedly and miserably at the carpet.

'Nurse Sellers.' His voice was as sharp as a whiplash. 'You are not paid to sit in the dining-room drinking coffee. I am sure you have been told that your patients are your first consideration and should and must have your undivided attention. There is no place at Highfields for a nurse who does not keep that rule. Whether or not in future you will be permitted to take coffee when you are on duty depends on Sister Mailer. At the moment I am too angry to venture a ruling. You may go,' he ended harshly.

The walk to the door over the thick-piled carpet seemed endless as she made her way to it on shaking legs. Once outside in the corridor she wiped her eyes and blew her nose and told herself fervently that she hated him. How dare he speak to me like that? she repeated over and over again to herself. There was no need for him to be so hateful. Anyhow she had done him a good turn, hadn't she? If Winston's stay was to be prolonged he would benefit financially and she was quite sure he would not object to that.

As she continued sorting through the linen she remembered with a feeling of horror that it was tomorrow that she was going out with him and Wendy. She buried her face in her hands.

'I can't go, I can't possibly go,' she said aloud, clenching her fists so that her nails cut into the palms of her hands.

When she was off duty she walked home around the esplanade and breathed deeply of the salt air. She leaned against the railings and listened to the sea as it dragged back the shingle then returned with a muted thud to swoosh up the beach then recede again. The only people on the esplanade were walking briskly as if on their way home. There were lights in the cottages at the base of St

Michael's Mount and also in the castle on the summit. What a strange peaceful life that would be, to live there and be of the world and yet apart from it. She wondered what kind of man lived in the castle. Did he have a family of children who played around the ramparts, whose voices echoed in the tall rooms? Or was he a private person who lived alone, the solitary life of a hermit? Lights had sprung up in the houses along the coast road making it look like a jewelled bracelet. Everywhere was beautiful and peaceful. Reluctantly she dragged herself away to return to Harbour View for the evening meal.

There was a savoury smell of cooking in the house and the attractive sound of crockery and cutlery being moved.

'Hello Nurse, had a good day?' Mrs Rosewall emerged from the kitchen and went in the dining-room.

'Yes thank you. And you? Something smells delicious.'

She went upstairs to wash and change and when she came down again the others were already seated at the table.

Talk was easy, both Mrs Rosewall and Janice, her daughter, recounting incidents of their day. After supper they watched television for a while, then Bryony and Janice went out for a walk across the esplanade, where people were still meandering along, or leaning on the railings to enjoy the beauty of the scenery—the moon which sent a golden ripple across the sea, and the floodlit castle which surmounted the Mount. There was a feeling of silence despite the sound of the waves as they broke on the beach.

Janice was a quiet girl and after a while she said, quite surprisingly,

'Is anything the matter, Bryony?'

'No, not really,' Bryony replied. 'But I'm in a bit of a quandary. I have had an offer—it's quite a fabulous one, really, so I suppose I should be over the moon—but I don't know . . .'

'Would you like to talk about it?'

'Well, one of our patients—she's very wealthy—has asked me to go and live with her as a sort of nurse-companion when she leaves Highfields, which should be any time now. Apparently she has a lovely home, near Falmouth I think, and a staff of servants. She has offered to double my salary and buy me a car for my own use, which is quite super . . .'

'I should say it is! So why are you hesitating?'

Bryony moved uncomfortably. 'I don't know whether to accept or not. And I haven't got long to make up my mind.'

'I shouldn't have thought it needed much thinking about. That's if you like the woman, of course.'

Bryony realised that she had not given that aspect much thought.

'Since you mention it, I must admit she is not my favourite person, although she is always very pleasant to me. But not to everybody. She can be autocratic and she's certainly a bit of a hypochondriac as well.'

'Why is she in Highfields? What is her trouble?'

'You tell me! She seems in the pink as far as I can see. But she has been there for ages, it must have cost her a fortune by now.'

'Of course it would be very lonely for you, cooped up with one woman who thought she was an invalid,' Janice said thoughtfully. 'Would you mind that? I should have thought you were more for company. I know I should be.'

'Yes, well I suppose that is why I'm not sure what I want to do. In a way I'd rather stay at Highfields, but there are not very many people working there and so if one of them is nasty to you it's pretty rotten,' Bryony said wistfully.

Janice looked at her in surprise. 'Of course you get that sometimes wherever you work. Who is nasty to you there, then?'

Bryony shrugged. 'It was my own fault really. I neglected one of the patients, quite inadvertently, but it has possibly set him back a bit.' She ran her tongue across her lips. 'Dr Crosland was furious with me, I thought he was going to give me the sack. Anyone would have thought that I deliberately set out to ruin his career.'

'Dr Crosland? Oh I know, is he that very good-looking chap who goes around with a red-haired woman?'

Bryony nodded.

'I shouldn't worry about that. He had probably

just had a row with her. You know what tempers red-heads are supposed to have. He was venting his feelings on you.'

That solution, though kindly meant, did nothing to soothe Bryony's feelings. She felt utterly miserable.

'And I hope that you don't leave. Mum and I would miss you.'

'And I would miss you,' Bryony admitted.

'Well, if you ask my opinion I'd say stick it out at Highfields. You haven't been there any time yet. You can't keep chopping and changing just because someone speaks to you sharpish.'

'No, I suppose not,' Bryony said thoughtfully.

But she gave an inner sigh. It was not as straightforward a problem as she had made it out to be.

CHAPTER SIX

BRYONY had prayed for rain but when she awoke after an uncomfortable and restless night the sun was shining from a cloudless sky.

I can say that I'm ill, she thought. Then she dismissed the idea. She would not put it past Dr Crosland to come and examine her and as there would be no prospect of her paying for accommodation at Highfields she would be pronounced fit in no uncertain manner, probably be yanked from her bed and made to dress and accompany them on this day's outing which she was so dreading.

Surely she could refuse to go? Was there any reason why he should tell her what she must do? The answers came immediately. No, she could not refuse to go, and yes, he could tell her what she must do, because he was lord and master of Highfields, and all who sailed in her! I hate him, I really do hate him—he is arrogant, bad-tempered and money-grabbing, she told herself over and over again.

She crawled unwillingly from her bed and gave serious thought as to what she should wear. She went over to the window and opening it put her head outside to decide whether it was going to be as hot as the last few days. She thought that it was and that she would be quite justified in wearing a thin cream silk dress which she had bought for her honeymoon and not yet worn. It was sleeveless and had a low, scalloped neckline and was buttoned through with dainty gold filigree buttons. It represented almost a month's salary and Bryony had a moment's hesitation when she wondered about Wendy's possibly grubby fingers. I'll face that problem if it happens, she decided, fastening the narrow gilt belt. After trying on various pieces of costume jewellery and discarding them, she settled on wearing a small cream and coral silk square which she tied around her neck.

If she had not been certain that she was looking her best, her reception at breakfast would have reassured her.

'That's a lovely dress, Nurse.' Mrs Rosewall placed the milk jug on the table and came closer to get a better look.

'It's pure silk, isn't it? It seems too good for every day wear. You should keep it for a special occasion.'

It had been bought for a special occasion. Bryony had a fleeting imaginary picture of herself and Nick having breakfast in the Bournemouth hotel they had chosen for their honeymoon. At the thought the shame and hurt of his rejection was sharp within her. Would he and Pamela go to that hotel? Not likely! Pamela Cutts would undoubtedly choose somewhere like the Seychelles or Miami, and

Daddy would foot the bill. Her thoughts went to Dr Crosland and she wondered why he was still single. Soon, rumour had it, that would be remedied if Dr Thea Browne had her way. She choked over her tea. Oh well, she wished them joy of each other but she could not imagine that it would be a very comfortable arrangement. Fancy being married to him! Or to her. They probably deserved each other.

She was to meet him outside his house at half past ten and the time was dragging. She went up to her room and brushed her hair yet again. Then she touched her cheeks with blusher for she was looking pale. She could see in the mirror that her eyes were as dark as unpolished pewter and knew that always happened when she was feeling especially tense. She leaned forward to colour her lips but her hand shook so much that she had to wipe it off and start again.

When she had done she tilted her small chin and tossed back the fair hair from her face. I am only fiddling with my appearance until it's time to leave, not for any other reason, she assured herself. Then she turned quickly away before her reflection could jeer at her.

Ellis Crosland was looking ridiculously handsome in a light beige safari suit. Bryony approached him on feet that felt too heavy to lift. Her heart was beating so loudly that she could hear it in her ears and it blotted out all other sounds.

His eyes travelled slowly over her as they took in

every smallest detail of her appearance. She swallowed twice, licked her lips, and said in a voice which came out as a whisper,

'Good morning sir.'

'Good morning Nurse. It's another lovely day.'

Wendy slammed the door and came running down the steps towards them. She slipped her hand in Bryony's, and swung their arms to and fro.

'Hello Nurse. I wonder where we're going? I'm glad you're coming too.'

Dr Crosland opened the passenger door of the car and as Bryony climbed in to it, her body brushed against his. Immediately every nerve throbbed into life, and robbed her limbs of their strength. Their eyes met briefly and there was an awareness in his which told her that he knew the effect he had on her. The blood which could so easily colour her cheeks did so now, and she turned away in embarrassment.

He opened the door for Wendy then walked around the car and took his place beside Bryony. He leaned against the steering-wheel and half turned towards her.

'I thought that we might go to the Lizard area. It is very lovely around there—Kynance and Mullion—they are all well-known beauty spots. What do you say? Do you know that part of Cornwall?'

She looked down at her hands which were tightly clenched on her lap.

'No sir, I don't know Cornwall at all. It sounds lovely.'

'Right. Then that's what we will do.'

He switched on the ignition, gave a fleeting glance to make sure that her seat belt was fastened, turned to wink reassuringly at Wendy, then the engine came alive and they purred away up the road which led to the town centre.

It was market day. Farmers and their wives stood in groups discussing crops and prices and family news with neighbouring farmers, it was a weekly meeting they all enjoyed. The market house was noisy with the sound of buying and selling. This was where the country people did their weekly shopping before loading it up in their cars to take home. Stalls had been set up outside displaying home-grown fruit and vegetables and buckets full of bright, assorted country flowers.

On the opposite side of the road visitors stood outside the Post Office sticking stamps on holiday postcards and there was a general air of festivity as they took pictures of the scene and of the statue of Sir Humphrey Davy, the Cornishman who invented the miners' safety lamp, which stood impressively before the market house.

They followed the road out of the town which ran beside the sea and led to Marazion. The tide was out and visitors were settling themselves on the sandy beach. A few people were walking along the causeway which led to the Mount. Dr Crosland stopped the car so that they could view it at close quarters.

'I should have liked to have taken you both

across to the Mount but it is not open to visitors on Thursdays.'

'Where are those people going then, Uncle?'

'They're going across but they can only walk around the base by the harbour and village store. There's little point in doing that. You want to go over the castle. It used to be a Benedictine priory in the eleventh century, then it was combined with a royal castle. It's National Trust now, but before that it changed hands many times over the centuries. During the Cornish revolt in 1549 it was the scene of a great deal of fighting.'

'It is really so beautiful with all those dark green trees and vegetation. It looks far too serene to have had wars there.'

'And when has war been a respector of places?' he asked wryly. 'Under the floor of the castle chapel the skeleton of a giant was unearthed just over a hundred years ago. You didn't know we had real giants down here in Cornwall, did you, Wendy?'

'Giants, Uncle Ellis? Will you take us there another day? Will we be able to see one?'

He laughed. 'I'll certainly take you there, but I can't promise to show you a giant.'

They drove on through country lanes where the hedges were bright with pink campions and white wild parsley.

Bryony gave a gasp of delight. 'Just look at those hedges! They're beautiful. All pink and white. I don't imagine that people up country have any idea that there are hedges like these. I know I hadn't. Aren't they pretty, Wendy?'

'When I was quite little I was a bridesmaid. Did you know that, Uncle Ellis? I wore a pink and white dress.' After a moment she added, 'I don't think I looked very much like these hedges. Not really.'

'Do you like living in Cornwall?' Ellis asked.

Bryony thought of London and the happy times she had had there with Nick. When they could afford it they went to the theatre, and when they had a free day they visited the zoo or art galleries or museums. Many a fine day they had spent in one or other of the parks. And St Stephen's had been a hive of industry, like a small town with its numerous departments, clinics and offices. She thought nostalgically of her many friends there and the variety of patients, of the dances and garden-parties and jumble sales which were held by the Friends of the hospital. And of her parents and home. She was silent for so long that Dr Crosland turned to look down at her and she saw for the first time that there were flecks of green in his honey-coloured eyes. She was fascinated by them and felt she could have looked into them for ever.

She knew that he was waiting for her to answer.

'I—I like it very much. The scenery is fantastic. But it is very different from London. Everything is so much quieter and slower and—and somehow lonely,' she said at last.

'But it is easy to be lonely in a crowd, so they say.'

'I didn't find that, sir.'

He wrinkled up his forehead and gave her a sideways glance.

'As we are both off duty we can dispense with formalities, don't you think? Please call me by my name.'

'As you wish, Dr Crosland.'

'Not that,' he frowned. 'I dislike being called "doctor" when I'm away from the shop. People are inclined to tell me their symptoms to get my sympathy and free advice. Try "Ellis", will you?'

Bryony's mouth went dry. How could she call this autocratic man, whose word was law and who had yesterday practically wiped the floor with her, by his first name? Maybe she could compromise by not using any name at all.

'And what is your name, Nurse Sellers?'

She cleared her throat. 'It's Bryony.'

'Bryony? What a sweet-sounding name, and quite uncommon.' He glanced at her smooth, shining blonde hair and delicate features appreciatively.

'Thank you,' she murmured uneasily, and as they were just entering Helston, she said quickly, 'Isn't this where they hold the Furry dance?'

'That's right, on the eighth of May each year. The shops and offices remain closed and there is dancing in the streets all day long. In the morning the schoolchildren hold their dances and at midday the big wigs of the town have their turn and wear full morning dress, complete with toppers. It's quite fun. You must make a point of seeing it next year.'

Next year? She wondered briefly where she would be by then. She did not envisage a future for herself in Cornwall.

They were driving across a vast stretch of open heathland covered with gorse and heather.

'This is Goonhilly and that massive dish aerial is the satellite tracking station where we received the first television pictures from the United States via Telstar I,' Ellis said, slowing down.

'It's colossal, isn't it? It looks all wrong here. But what a marvellous invention, it makes my mind boggle.'

'Yes indeed. Quite near here is Poldhu where the Marconi Wireless Telegraphy station used to be. That was equally marvellous in its day. It is where the first morse signals were sent across the Atlantic and received from America.'

'All these marvellous inventions! Do you think they are a good thing? Sometimes I feel that people are becoming too clever. What will happen to these clever men when there is nothing left to discover?' Bryony said thoughtfully.

'Too clever? No! In medicine, as you know, there have been tremendous strides made, new cures, new preventatives for which we are all very grateful,' he said, turning down the road at Mullion which led to the Lizard.

'But we all have to die sometime. Does it make sense that old people should be kept alive although they are getting no enjoyment from life and might well prefer to be dead?'

'You sound as if you are in favour of euthanasia and I will tell you straight away that I am not. But this is neither the time nor the place for such a debate.' He braked and looked around. 'This seems to be a good spot for a picnic. Or would you prefer to have lunch in that hotel on the cliff? It is quite good there.'

Wendy pulled at Bryony's shoulder. 'Please say a picnic,' she whispered loudly.

Bryony glanced out of the window. 'Well I can't see anywhere that we could buy food. There aren't any shops here.'

Ellis laughed. 'My housekeeper fixed up a luncheon basket because Wendy was so full of the good time she had at St Ives. "We didn't go to a boring old hotel" she said. So we decided that a picnic would be the thing. But quite honestly I could not face another of those pasties! So what is it to be? The choice is yours.'

'Like Wendy, I should prefer the picnic,' she said.

He found a parking place, then unlocked the boot and took out a large wicker hamper.

'We'll walk along this path and see if we can find a suitable spot. We should be lucky for not many visitors come this way, it isn't well-known.'

The turf was green and springy, interspersed with rocks coloured in various shades of serpentine. Clumps of sea-pinks, prickly yellow gorse and blackthorn were set against the background of the aquamarine sea and the blue sky looked magical.

Ellis stopped and looked consideringly at some boulders which were set in a stretch of turf. 'What do you think? Will this suit you? Or would you prefer to be in the shade?'

Bryony sat down and leaned against a boulder. 'This is very comfortable. Do you like it here, Wendy?'

'Yes,' she said, and settled down beside her.

For a moment Bryony could hardly believe that this was real. That she, an unimportant nurse, was on this picnic with Dr Crosland, the formidable man who was either feared or adored by everyone with whom he came in contact.

'Shall we eat now, or later?'

Bryony recalled that she had been too nervous to eat anything at breakfast and had worried Mrs Rosewall by refusing anything but a cup of tea. Now she was suffering the pangs of hunger.

'Now please,' Wendy said quickly.

'Yes please. I'm starving,' Bryony agreed.

'It's most refreshing to hear young ladies wanting to eat. Most of them are het up with some slimming diet or other. And I don't approve of that.'

He opened the hamper which was attractively laid out in separate compartments.

'Mrs Hawkins has made us crab salad because it is Wendy's favourite dish. I hope you are not allergic to shellfish?'

'I don't think so.' She gave a cheeky grin. 'But if I

come out in a rash I have no doubt you will prescribe accordingly.

It had become hot since noon and as she removed the square of silk from her neck she saw Ellis's eyes alight and linger on the low scalloped neckline of her dress, and blushed.

'It would be criminal if such a thing were to occur,' he murmured.

The salad, with the coral of the crab nestling on wedges of iceberg lettuce, tomatoes and cucumber looked delicious. Ellis passed the mayonnaise and buttered split buns.

'I am very fortunate. I get presents of fish and crabs and lobsters from local fishermen and it tastes quite different from that you buy in shops.'

And if they catch a sturgeon, to whom do they first offer it? To you, or the Queen? Bryony thought wryly. She remembered the porter whom Ellis had thanked for fish on the day she arrived in Polwithy. She tried not to recall later telling him what a pompous and difficult man Dr Crosland was reputed to be.

'These are home-grown raspberries,' Ellis said, heaping sugar and clotted cream on them before passing them to her. 'Do you like them?'

'Rather! Do you grow them in your garden?'

'We do, but these were a present from an ex-patient.' His eyes twinkled. 'I get gifts from all and sundry. I believe it is the same for vicars. It is a very pleasant state of affairs.'

A ripe berry slipped from Bryony's fingers on to

the bodice of her dress and ran down, staining it red. She gave an exclamation of dismay.

Ellis bent across to look at it. 'We will do a little first aid treatment on that. But don't worry, if we can't get it out entirely take it in to the lab at Polwithy and they will attend to it.'

He took a linen napkin from the hamper, then paused thoughtfully.

'Wendy, would you be my assistant?'

'Yes please, Uncle. What shall I do? Oh dear, what a mess!'

'I want you to hold this inside Nurse's bodice so that I can rub it with some milk and salt. Will you do that?'

'This was my mother's favourite remedy,' he said, as he rubbed gently at the stain.

Bryony laughed to cover her embarrassment. 'I'm sure she would be pleased with this result. It's practically gone. Thanks very much.'

Wendy stared at the damp patch and said importantly,

'I think it prob'ly needs more treatment, Doctor. It isn't quite gone, not really.'

Ellis gave it another dab. 'It will no doubt dry out, Wendy. Shall we wait and see?'

Wendy jumped to her feet. 'Okay. I'll go and pick some flowers.'

'Don't go out of sight, Wendy. Do you want a drink before you go?'

She shook her head. 'No thanks.'

'A cup of coffee, Bryony?'

As she buttoned her bodice with shaking fingers she remembered with a sudden flash of resentment his treatment of her yesterday.

'Am I allowed to have any, sir?' she asked, tossing back her hair.

He looked at her consideringly, the flask poised in his hand.

'If you are referring to yesterday then I must remind you that I was extremely angry. It had been a hectic morning with the cardiac arrest scare, I glanced in at Deansborough believing him to be well on the road to recovery and found him in a very exhausted, distressed state. You deserved every word I said to you—and more, much more. You must understand that I will not tolerate inefficiency from any member of my staff, however lowly or exalted their position.'

Inefficiency! That settled it. She could not possibly stay on at Highfields if that was how he saw her.

'Mrs Trengwainton . . .' she began.

Now she would tell him that she wanted to leave the nursing home and take up the position she had been offered. That would show him that even if he did not think much of her as a nurse one of his wealthiest patients did. Should she also tell him that she would be paid twice her present salary? And be given a car?

'Mrs Trengwainton?' He wrinkled his forehead, and the corners of his mouth turned down.

He looked so desirable that she lacked the wish or the courage to continue her confession.

'Mrs Trengwainton seems so well, why don't you discharge her?' she asked instead.

The friendliness faded from his eyes and was replaced by the 'keep your distance' expression which she knew so much better. His voice was so severe that she cringed.

'Even if we were on duty I should have no intention whatsoever of discussing the treatment of one of my patients with you, or indeed with any other of the nurses. If I required a second opinion I might consult with Dr Browne. But the final decision is mine and mine alone. In any case, as I reminded you earlier on, we are off duty and I refuse to think or talk about work.'

He began to pack up their used dishes prior to throwing them in a litter bin.

Bryony bit her lip. Of course he would not discuss his wealthy patients' treatment, he would not risk being persuaded that they would be better off at home and so rob him of a few more weeks' high fees. She wondered whether he was so tardy in discharging patients from Polwithy General.

When everything was packed away and Wendy had returned with a bunch of wilting wild flowers clutched in her hand, Ellis decided that they should drive on to the Lizard. When they reached there Bryony thought it had hardly been worth the effort, for the only thing of interest was the lighthouse.

She stared around her with blank eyes.

'I brought you here because it is the most southerly place in Great Britain and when you return to London you will be able to boast to your friends that you have been here.' He looked at her mockingly. 'The lighthouse is one of the most powerful in the world, the reflections can be seen eighty miles away.'

'Oh good,' Bryony said flippantly, hurt at his casual reference to her possible departure.

'Okay, we will go the Lizard Town and you can enjoy yourself looking at the souvenirs like all the other tourists.'

It was just half a mile away and Ellis parked at the end of a long line of cars. The many small shops were crowded with visitors looking at clocks and ashtrays—anything made from the local serpentine.

Bryony searched among the souvenirs thinking that she would like to buy something for Wendy. She picked up a miniature lighthouse made in three shades of serpentine, red, green and grey.

'Would you like this, Wendy?' she asked.

Wendy stared at it thoughtfully. 'I'd rather have this,' she said, holding out a little brass pisky.

'Of course, it's much more fun. A little Cornish lucky pisky.'

She queued at the counter to pay for it and then they went back to the car and started for home.

When they neared Polwithy, the sun, a great red ball, was resting on the horizon, having left long scarlet streaks across the sky, reflected in the rippling sea. A red sky at night was supposed to herald a fine day tomorrow. But to Bryony tomorrow could not be better than today had been, for today was something she would always remember.

CHAPTER SEVEN

Dr Crosland was at a medical conference and Highfields seemed dull and lifeless. Time dragged. Even the patients were bored and disgruntled as if they were waiting for something to happen. And of course that was true. They were waiting for the return of the doctor whose presence brought warmth and cheer and vitality to the home.

Bryony carried out her duties mechanically. There were no new admissions and no patient was discharged. She thought of Wendy and pitied her for the loneliness of that large house which she felt certain would be empty without her Uncle Ellis.

Bryony was glad when she was off duty and could return to the pleasant boarding house, and she frequently congratulated herself on having secured such comfortable lodgings.

At supper one night Mrs Rosewall said,

'The Polwithy Players are doing *Dear Brutus* this week, Nurse. You really should go and see it, they always put on a good show, don't they, Janice?'

'Yes, we always look forward to them. They did *The Importance of Being Earnest* not long ago and that was ever so good, one of their best, I thought. Our friend, Mr Rippon, is in this one. He's taking the part of a butler. I know he's a bit pompous but I should have thought he would have had a more important part. He speaks up well.'

'Matey the butler is quite important. Don't you know the play? It's whimsical, of course, being Barrie.'

'No I don't know it. Mrs Davis, who works with me, said her niece is in it and she is still at school. She's got a big part,' Janice said.

'It's always fun to see a play when you know some of the people in it. We had a very good group at St Stephen's and some of the stuffiest doctors were excellent comedians. But I never felt quite the same about them afterwards. I found it difficult to take them seriously,' Bryony laughed.

'Were you in it?'

Bryony shook her head. 'No, I was too busy studying for my SRN. Not being all that bright it took me most of my time.'

She thought back to those days and knew that what she said was not strictly true, for she had spent nearly every spare moment with Nick.

'I should have thought they would have been after you to play the part of the leading lady,' Mrs Rosewall said, eyeing her fair hair and slim figure appreciatively.

'Me? I wouldn't have been any good, I'm far too easily embarrassed!'

'Why don't you come to *Dear Brutus* with us?' Janice suggested.

'That's very sweet of you, but I'm not sure if I can. You see when Dr Crosland comes back from the conference my duties may be altered, so I can't really make plans. I'm free tonight, though, if that's any good.'

'Tonight?' Mrs Rosewall said doubtfully. 'I'll just look at the TV programmes and see if there is anything on.'

She laid down the paper. 'Mostly repeats as usual, nothing I particularly want to see, so that settles it. But will we be able to get in at such short notice, Janice?'

'We should do if we get there early enough. At a pinch I could ask Mr Rippon, but I'd rather not.' She pulled a face.

They set off early. Bryony had changed quickly into a light grey dress in wild silk, with white trimmings and a large white collar. It was another garment from her trousseau, bought because of its virginal appearance. For despite the heavy petting that she and Nick had indulged in, despite the many occasions when she had been sorely tempted to agree to Nick becoming her lover, she had resisted the urge and was still a virgin. She had wanted desperately to keep something special for their honeymoon. Nick, she knew, had had many affairs with girls and she did not want to be another of them, she wanted to be his wife. Sometimes now her body craved for the satisfaction she had denied it, but in her heart she was thankful that she had waited, for if she had not, how much greater would the humiliation, the rejection and the shame have been.

'You look great in that, like a Quaker girl. You've got some super clothes,' Janice said admiringly.

Bryony squeezed her arm. 'You are a dear. You give a poor hard-working girl confidence.'

The Town Hall where the play was being performed was half a mile away. Bryony felt as if she was back at school as they walked along the narrow pavements, she and Mrs Rosewall in front and Janice following behind.

They arrived early, but such was the popularity of the local group it was only by a bit of juggling that they were able to get three seats together. Janice, who knew practically everybody in Polwithy, enjoyed herself telling Bryony who everybody was. The play was due to start and the doors had been shut. The audience put down their programmes and looked expectantly at the red velvet curtains. Suddenly a door was pushed open and the last person Bryony would have expected to see there entered and paused to buy a programme. It was Ellis, closely followed by Dr Browne. So he was back from the conference. His handsome face had taken on a slight tan since that day they had lain in the sun and an ache started inside Bryony and gripped her heart relentlessly, spoiling the evening for her before it had even started.

She watched as they made their way to their seats. Thea was dressed in deep blue which complemented the colour of her hair, she looked like a flame in a dreary street, making everybody nearby seem drab. She dropped her stole and Ellis bent to pick it up. As he straightened up he glanced at the people in the rows behind and his eyes alighted on Bryony.

At the same moment Mrs Rosewall said, 'Oh, there's Dr Crosland and his girlfriend. It's about time they named the day, they've been going around together for a very long time, haven't they, Janice?'

If James Barrie had still been alive he would have been justifiably outraged to have known that there was a young woman in the audience who had no interest whatsoever in his play. She laughed and clapped when the others did but what she saw was Ellis and Thea Browne. She saw when he bent his head to make some remark to her or listen to something she had to say, she saw his profile, the strong nose, the square chin and the lock of nut-brown hair that fell over his forehead. She saw the set of his eyes and the lines that radiated from their corners and the compressed mouth which suddenly smiled. And she knew that the smile would be sweet and tender for there would be no aloofness nor condemnation in it for Dr Browne.

When the lights went up after the first act Bryony was amazed. She realised that she could have seen none of those things from where she was sitting, they were all in her imagination.

'It's good, isn't it? Are you enjoying it, Nurse?' Mrs Rosewall asked.

'Yes, very much. They are all excellent. It is well

cast,' Bryony replied with forced enthusiasm.

During the next act Bryony became aware that Janice was having difficulty in breathing as she tried to stifle a fit of coughing.

Mrs Rosewall got to her feet. 'She's got an attack of asthma coming on. Let me pass.'

Bryony laid a detaining hand on her arm. 'No,' she whispered, 'You stay here. I'll see to her.'

She followed Janice into the foyer. 'Have you got a puffer?'

Janice wheezed and shook her head, unable to speak.

'I've got some aspirin. Are you able to take that?'

She could only nod her head.

A young man who had followed them out fetched a glass of water at Bryony's request and at last the attack subsided a little.

'I—I'll be all right now. You go back, Nurse, I'll just sit out here.'

'No, I don't want to go back. If you know of a café nearby a cup of coffee sometimes helps.'

By the time they reached one Janice was very much better.

'Do you know what brought it on?'

'No, I've no idea. I haven't had an attack for ages. I thought I might have grown out of it.'

'I wonder what triggered this off?'

Janice grinned. 'Perhaps someone had a cat pushed up her jumper.'

'Seriously, are cats the trouble? Because someone may have been wearing a fur they thought was fox!'

'I honestly don't know. It could have been something I ate, I suppose.'

'What does your GP say it is?'

Janice frowned. 'Oh I haven't asked him, it isn't worth bothering about, I get it so seldom. I'm only sorry that I've spoilt the evening for you.'

'Don't be, I don't mind in the least. But I do think you should have a word with your doc, that's what he's for.'

When it was time for the show to end they walked back to meet Mrs Rosewall. As they waited outside the Town Hall for her to come out Bryony's heart leapt. Ellis Crosland passed so close to her that she could have put out her hand and touched him. As if he knew she was there he suddenly looked straight at her, then paused.

'Is everything all right?' His honey-gold eyes looked concerned.

Bryony flushed. 'Yes, thank you. My friend had an attack of asthma but she is all right now.'

Ellis turned and looked at Janice as if he was noting everything about her, her slightly rounded shoulders, pale face and heavy eyes.

He gave her a reassuring smile. 'Good.' Then he rejoined Thea.

She murmured something to him and they both laughed. Bryony felt weak with envy.

Mrs Rosewall came bustling up to them. 'Are you all right now, Janice? I was thinking—I hope it wasn't those prawns we had that upset you?'

'No Mum, I've had attacks other times without eating shellfish.'

'It could be the scent I'm wearing—it's new,' Bryony suggested.

Janice frowned. 'I'm all right now, so let's forget it. How did the play go?'

By the time they reached home every performance had been praised or criticised. Bryony tried to appear interested but her mind was on Ellis and the woman he was going to marry. Thea Browne, a clever doctor with a superb figure and magnificent hair. And one day she would have everything.

Lucky Thea Browne.

CHAPTER EIGHT

Mrs Chamberlain, a diabetic, had been admitted because of the side effects she suffered from insulin.

'How do you feel today?' Bryony asked as she made her bed.

The patient was sitting in a chair beside the french doors which led out into the garden.

'Marvellous, Nurse. Your Dr Crosland is a miracle-worker.'

'So they tell me,' Bryony said drily. 'And what miracle has he performed for you?'

'Well to tell you the truth I didn't think I was long for this world. I couldn't live without insulin and it was making me feel so ill I didn't think I could live *with* it, either. So a friend told me to see Dr Crosland and it was the best thing I ever did.'

Bryony thumped the pillows. 'Tell me more,' she said.

'Well, he told me to come in to Highfields and he would see what he could do for me. Honestly I was reluctant to do that. I knew that it would be very expensive and I didn't think he would be able to help me. But he's got such a way with him, just looking at him gave me confidence. So to cut a long story short I did come in and he put me on synthetic insulin and I feel another woman. My eyes had been so bad I thought I was going blind, now they don't bother me at all. And I haven't had nearly so much pain in my legs. I can't tell you how delighted I am.'

'That's splendid, I'm very glad it works for you. Now, do you want to get back into bed? Or would you rather sit out for the time being?'

'I'll stay here, Nurse, it's so lovely with the sun and the garden and the sea. I know it's costing a fortune for me to be here but as far as I am concerned it is worth every penny.'

'So you are a satisfied customer in fact,' Bryony smiled as she went out of the room.

She went next to Mrs Andrewartha who was now recovering from her pleurisy.

'I'm getting on fine, Nurse, thanks to your Dr Crosland. Isn't he a heart-throb? How can you girls manage to stop yourselves from falling in love with him?'

Bryony gave a wry smile. 'We work at it,' she said.

'And he is so kind and caring! Nothing is too much trouble and if you're feeling low and need someone to talk to you would think he had all the time in the world to spare. Different from my doctor who has a stop-watch when you go in his surgery and when your time is up out you go. Not for one moment does Dr Crosland let you feel you are talking too much or are a nuisance.'

Because, unlike with your GP, you are paying handsomely for his services, Bryony thought.

'Yes, he is a good doctor,' she agreed coolly.

Mrs Andrewartha looked at her with curiosity. 'Is that all you can say? Haven't you fallen for him?'

'It wouldn't do any good if I had, Mrs Andrewartha. I'm just a nurse and he more or less owns this place besides being a top consultant. We are as far apart as the poles.'

'I suppose so. But human feelings must come into it as well. You are an exceptionally pretty girl if you don't mind my saying so.'

'Not at all,' Bryony laughed. 'Keep on talking.'

'I'm sure you don't need me to tell you that. But I expect you have got a young man, haven't you?'

'Nobody serious. Now, have you got everything you want?' Bryony opened the windows beside the doors and drew back the curtains. 'You aren't in a draught, are you?'

'No thank you, that's lovely. Will my pin-up be paying me a visit this morning?'

'You mean your husband?'

'No, silly! I mean Dr Crosland who we've been talking about.'

'Oh—I expect so. Shall I tell him what you have been saying about him?' Bryony asked mischievously.

'Don't you dare embarrass the dear man. I know that I can never have him but I can have my dreams,' she smiled.

That makes two of us, Bryony thought, as she

continued on her way along the corridor. There are so many women in love with him but only one can have him. Dr Browne with her slim, elegant figure and magnificent hair.

Winston Deansborough was sitting by the window reading. He smiled brilliantly when Bryony entered.

'Hello Nurse, how are you?' His teeth looked very white against his dark skin.

'I'm well thank you. But more to the point, how are you?'

His smile faded. 'To what point is that, please?'

'Just a saying, Mr Deansborough. How are you?'

'I am damn fine, I can use this elbow crutch splendidly. You told me I could do it with practise and you were right.'

'But I didn't mean you to do too much all at once. You got over-tired, didn't you?' Bryony reproved him gently.

He laughed. 'Yes, I did too much, I was knocked out. Dr Crosland was so angry, I have never seen a man more angry. I was so scared! But all is now well, I am forgiven. Soon I will be leaving you.'

'Splendid! I'm very glad for you. So now you can walk without your crutch?'

'No, I have not done that yet. You want I should try?'

Bryony looked alarmed. 'Oh no, please! Don't try until Dr Crosland says you may.'

'I will say you gave me permission. How will that be?'

'Disastrous,' Bryony said firmly. 'If you say that I'll get the sack.'

'That I cannot believe.'

'Really, I am not able to give you permission. Only Dr Crosland can prescribe treatment.'

'Okay. When I see him today I will ask him. Is that right?'

'Yes, that's the thing to do.'

After she had completed her round Bryony went to the dining-room for coffee as Sister Mailer had not made it out of bounds for her. She was pleased to see Rene there looking big and warm and smiling.

'Hello stranger,' Bryony said as she joined her.

Nurse Dyson squinted at her as if she could barely recognise her. 'It's the new nurse from London, isn't it? The one who pinches all the cushy jobs.'

'Cushy jobs? What are they for goodness' sake?'

'What are they? she asks. Those trips out with—afraid I can't get up to curtsey—Dr Crosland.'

'Oh those. I was only acting as nursemaid to Wendy,' Bryony said.

'He hasn't taken you with them today, then?'

'Today? I don't think he's off today. Quite a lot of patients have put on their best nighties in preparation for his visit,' Bryony said.

'Then you can nip back and tell them they can take them off again for he set off in the car with Wendy.'

'Did he?'

Rene eyed her over the rim of her cup. 'Dr Browne was with them.'

Bryony felt as if she had stepped off a step that was not there. She took a sip of coffee and noticed that it tasted like senna tea.

'Then perhaps Wendy isn't very well and that is why she went with them.'

Rene threw back her head and laughed. 'If you believe that you'll believe anything. No, my child, they are in love. It wouldn't surprise me if they had gone shopping to buy the ring.'

'With Wendy?' Bryony asked weakly.

'Of course with Wendy. She is the chaperon. People in their positions don't want to have the finger pointed at them. Not that I can imagine either of them rolling in the hay.'

Bryony noticed her friend's bulging waist and brawny arms and wondered crossly why she didn't diet. Then she pushed the unkind thought aside and concentrated on her own future.

She had been avoiding Mrs Trengwainton so that she need not yet make a decision. Now, however, she could put it off no longer. When Ellis and Thea were married, Highfields would be no better than a prison to her. She was extremely lucky that she had had this offer from Mrs Trengwainton. She would have practically no work to do, a large salary and a car. The days would be dull, however, and she would miss Mrs Rosewall and Janice, for there would only be Mrs Trengwainton's company and her conversation would centre almost completely on herself and her health—or ill-health. She would also miss Rene. Her mind wavered. Should she go or should she stay? If she went she knew that she most probably would never see Ellis again and that seemed unbearable. But could she tolerate seeing him and knowing that he belonged to Thea Browne? She sighed heavily, unaware that she had done so, until Rene said robustly.

'You're only one of many women who have fallen under his spell. It's rumoured here that a patient once tried to commit suicide because of him.'

Bryony's eyes flew wide open. 'Oh I don't believe that.'

'Suit yourself. Of course it turned out she was a nutter. Well, she must have been to have done that.'

'What do you think of him?' Bryony asked curiously, knowing that she had a boyfriend and wondering whether she was so in love with him that Ellis failed to attract her.

'Me?' She stretched out her hefty legs and folded her arms across her comfortable chest. 'I don't box out of my class. I'd be a mug to drool over a man who would not be interested in me in a million years. That is one of the benefits of being plain and knowing you are. Now with a pretty girl like yourself you could have a secret hope that you had a chance.'

'So you think that all men, even the clever ones, go for looks?'

'Not when you see some of their wives! But looks go a long way if they are after an affair. And let's face it, they are only human. Sorry Dr Crosland.' She crossed herself. 'I wasn't meaning you. But they do work very hard and such long hours, and they have such a tremendous lot of stress and responsibility it is only to be expected that they like to unwind with a pretty girl. When it comes to choosing a wife, of course, that's another kettle of fish.'

Bryony was silent, thinking over what Rene had said. Maybe in time she could become Ellis Crosland's 'pretty girl', and be rewarded with a meal and a car ride. But it was Thea Browne whom he would ask to marry him.

It seemed that all men were out for the best they could get for themselves. Like Nick. He had tossed her aside when he met someone with more to offer him, someone with money and status. And he had not cared at all about the misery and loss she had suffered. Indeed she doubted if he had given her a second thought. Yet they had been so close, so much in love.

'With Dr Browne she would have both looks and wife material to offer,' she said flatly.

'You never spoke a truer word.' Rene stood up and sent a shower of cake crumbs on to the carpet. 'But our Dr Crosland is no fool, he knows that he can have whoever he wants and Dr Browne, so far, is the best bet. Mind you, he is a long time popping the question. Maybe he is looking around to make sure he isn't missing someone with even more to offer. Like a millionairess beauty queen with a titled father.'

Bryony turned aside in distress. 'You make him sound so cold-blooded, but I suppose you could be right. That's what men are like.'

'Not all of them, thank goodness, else who would look at plain mortals like me, without money, status or looks? But I've got me a smashing fellow and if I had any of those virtues I might think he wanted me for that only. As it is, it must be the me inside me that he loves.'

'And so he should,' Bryony said warmly. 'It is only in your own eyes that you are plain.'

Rene laid a large, hot hand on Byrony's shoulder. 'I'm a realist. I know what I am and who I am and I don't expect or want to move out of my station in life. Take my advice—never throw your love away on a man who has got everything and who thinks a lot of himself, because it can only lead to heartbreak. Pick someone who will appreciate you for what you are and be proud of you. There must be plenty like that around.' She winked at Bryony and plodded out of the room.

Bryony closed her eyes against the ache of tears. Rene's advice made sense, it was a waste of emotion to expend it on someone who did not reciprocate. But how to control those feelings and to fall in love with someone as ordinary as oneself was an impossibility.

She wondered where Ellis and Thea had gone

today. Would they be having a picnic? Or lunching in a hotel? She wondered if they were lovers. She had never considered herself to be a particularly jealous person, but what was this tenseness in her head, the ache in her heart, the fierce longing, if it were not jealousy?

CHAPTER NINE

It was almost visiting time and Bryony was seeing that her patients were comfortable and had everything they needed before they arrived. Being a private nursing home, theoretically visitors could come when they pleased, but there was an unwritten law that mornings were kept free for Dr Crosland to speak to his patients, and for necessary treatment.

'Nurse,' Rosemary Boase called as Bryony was about to leave. 'Can you spare a few minutes please?'

Bryony returned to her bedside with a pleasant smile for the thin-faced young woman with the anxious frown. 'Certainly, Mrs Boase. What can I do for you?'

Rosemary plucked at the sheet with nervous fingers. 'I—I don't like to say anything because everybody is so kind—and—it's lovely here. But the truth is—I can't really afford to go on staying here. I was wondering if I could be moved to Polwithy General for my operation, and have it on the NHS?' She gave a quick embarrassed glance at Bryony, then looked down at her hands again.

'What operation is that, Mrs Boase?'

'Why—my duodenal ulcer,' she said in a surprised voice.

'Has Dr Crosland said that you will be having surgery?'

'No, he hasn't mentioned it yet, but I would like to leave here before he does.'

'What makes you think that you will be having an operation?'

'Because my cousin did when she had an ulcer. And you do, don't you?'

'Well I am not qualified to say what will happen, but nowadays they only operate for duodenal ulcers in certain cases. There is a new drug which is very good indeed. It's cimetidine and can clear up an ulcer like magic.'

Mrs Boase looked unconvinced. 'I'm fed up with drugs and medicines, I'd rather they operated and got rid of it once and for all.'

'I can understand how you feel but this new drug is really something. They now think that an ulcer can be caused by a virus and this drug attacks the virus. That's all I know about it. But worrying isn't going to do it any good, whatever the cause, so why don't you speak to Dr Crosland about it? Explain your financial position to him,' Bryony suggested.

'Oh I couldn't say that to him!'

'Why not? Most people say that he is exceptionally understanding.'

'He is, and that is just why I wouldn't like to mention it. It would look as if now that I've had his advice I want the treatment for free.'

'I don't think he would look at it that way,' Bryony said.

'You see, we only reckoned on paying him for the consultation, we never dreamed I would be coming in here. It's Brian I feel sorry for. He's so good and kind but he doesn't earn a lot.'

'I understand. I know it costs the earth in here. I think the best thing you can do is to have a word with Sister Mailer and she can speak to Dr Crosland. All right?'

Rosemary nodded and sighed. 'Thank you, I'll do that. You are all so kind it makes me feel dreadful having to ask.'

Bryony was off duty now. She went to the changing-room and unpinned her dainty pleated cap with the pink streamers, took off her uniform dress and apron and changed into her comfortable blue jeans and open-necked check shirt. She ran a comb through her silky hair, slung her bag over her shoulder and walked down the corridor to the front door. She had almost reached it when it was suddenly flung open and she came face to face with Ellis. As always her heart zoomed up and then slid down again. She glanced at him shyly and noticed the strained look of anxiety on his face.

'Have you seen Wendy?' he asked abruptly.

'Wendy? No, I haven't, sir. Has she been here?'

'That's what I wanted to know. I left her at Polwithy General with Dr Browne and now she is nowhere to be found.'

'Perhaps she has gone home?' Bryony suggested.

He shook his head. 'I've just been there but Mrs Hawkins hasn't seen her.' For the first time since she had known him, he seemed uncertain what to do next.

'I'm off duty now, would you like me to go to the hospital to look for her? There must be lots of places there where she could be.' Bryony felt an overwhelming urge to smooth the worry lines from his forehead and the anxiety from his eyes.

'Thank you but there are several nurses already doing that. They have been searching for some time,' he added bleakly.

'Has she ever run away before?'

'No. Well sometimes she has hidden for a few minutes, but only in the house.' He ran a finger around inside his collar. 'I don't know where to look next. She has never been out on her own since she came to us so she doesn't know the district at all.'

'I should think that the beach or the town would be the most likely places. Shall I go down to the beach first? If she is there it should be easy to spot her.'

He nodded. 'We'll go together and if she isn't there we will drive to the town.'

They crossed the esplanade in silence and stopped at the railings to scan the beach. Bryony had forgotten the many huge boulders and rocks when she said it would be easy to see Wendy if she were there.

'I'll run down and ask someone if they've seen

her,' she said, and went down the long flight of narrow stone steps.

The young couple she approached were engrossed in one another and annoyed at being disturbed. They looked at her with unfriendly suspicion.

'No, we haven't seen anyone like that. All we've seen are those boys over there.'

She thanked them and picked her way over the pebbles to two young boys who were skimming flints over the water. They listened to Bryony and grinned at each other.

'Yes, I seen her,' the younger one said.

'No you haven't, we ain't seen no one,' his friend said belligerently.

'Yes I have.'

'No you haven't.'

They started fighting and laughing and rolling on the stones and Bryony knew that she would get no more information from them.

She looked behind boulders and in all directions in vain, then ran back up the steps.

'No luck,' she said. 'Not on this part of the beach anyhow.'

'Thank you for asking. We'll walk on to the end, shall we?'

The beach appeared to be completely deserted. 'I can't take up any more of your time, Nurse, I'll drive up to the town now.'

'My time is my own so I'll come too if you'd like me to.'

He gave her a brief, grateful smile. 'That's good

of you. We will drop in at Polwithy first in case she has turned up there.'

'How long has she been missing? Bryony asked as they drove towards the hospital.

Ellis glanced at the watch on his wrist. 'I don't know. It's about two hours since we discovered that she had gone but when she actually left is anyone's guess.'

'Didn't Dr Browne know?'

'Apparently not. She very kindly agreed to let Wendy stay with her because my housekeeper had to go out, but of course she had her patients to attend to and couldn't be expected to watch her every minute.'

If I had been minding Wendy and she wandered away I bet he wouldn't have made excuses for me, she thought resentfully.

'I should think she is definitely somewhere in the hospital. It's a big place to a small girl, she could easily lose her way. I frequently did when I first went to St Stephen's,' Bryony confided.

'Let's hope you're right.' He parked outside the hospital. 'If you wouldn't mind waiting here, Nurse, I shan't be gone long.'

Bryony stared at all the cars parked around her. She tried to imagine where she would go if she were a child like Wendy. She had no friends whom she might have called on and knew nothing of her surroundings. When they had walked around the shops at St Ives Wendy had not shown much interest in them so it was hard to imagine that she would walk the quite considerable distance from the hospital to the town. It seemed far more likely that she was either in the hospital somewhere or hidden by the boulders on the beach. She could think of nowhere else.

Ellis came towards her looking desperately worried. He shook his head briefly.

'I should be seeing my patients now. Thea is standing in for me again, it's extremely good of her.'

'If you want to get back to work I will go on looking for Wendy,' Bryony said.

'That is most kind but we can cover more ground by car. And I would rather not see my patients at all than not be able to give them my full attention.'

'I've been thinking. Wendy isn't all that keen on shops, so unless she had something she particularly wanted to buy I doubt if she would go to the town. Would she have wanted to buy a birthday present or something special for herself?'

Ellis hesitated, his long, capable fingers resting on the steering-wheel. He considered for a moment, then shook his head.

'No, there are no birthdays coming up and I can't think she would go shopping for something for herself. She would have no hesitation in asking me if she could have it.'

'There was quite a stretch of beach where she could have been hidden from sight. Perhaps she's there,' Bryony suggested.

'I can't imagine anyone wanting to stay for long on Polwithy beach, there's nothing there to occupy a child. But she must be somewhere. Now that we are here we will continue through the town, go round by the harbour and back across the esplanade. If we haven't found her by then I will drop in at the police station.'

It was late and most of the shops had closed. A few shoppers with laden baskets plodded towards home. There was a dismal air in the town. Litter was on the pavements and in the gutters and the cars that had earlier lined the sides of the street had so depleted in number that it looked empty. Ellis drove slowly and they were both silent as they scanned the pavements and openings to side-streets for a small girl with her hair tied in a pony-tail and wearing, according to Ellis, a blue and white spotted dress.

They came to the harbour and looked with dread at the quay which had no railings to stop an unwary pedestrian from falling into the deep water between the many boats anchored there. And probably no one would see or notice the tiny splash that a child might make. Further along there were cargo boats which might entice a child to go aboard to find out where all the crates were stored.

Bryony was glad when they turned the corner which led to the esplanade, although on the opposite side of the road there was a small pleasure garden and behind it a graveyard where recently a rapist had lurked.

'We'll try this end of the beach,' Ellis said, as he parked by the kerb.

They walked until they came to another flight of steps which led to the beach. Here they separated to make their search. The beach seemed deserted for as far as you could see, except for a scruffy-looking mongrel who stood by the water's edge and stared out to sea. It was half-tide. The water was grey over the pebbles and the waves rolled mournfully over the beach without any frivolous, dancing spray.

Bryony looked at the dog and wondered if he had come here on his own or if there was a master nearby. She scrunched her way around some boulders hoping and yet fearing that she would see someone lurking there. Suddenly she heard some pebbles move and looked around for Ellis but he had wandered further along the beach. The dog cocked an ear and ran towards the steps. As it neared them Bryony saw a flash of blue which immediately disappeared behind a rock. She hurried up the beach hopefully, the pebbles slipping back under her feet.

'Wendy!' she called.

There was no reply. 'Wendy!' she called again, as she drew nearer the rocks.

The little girl was sitting in a niche which rendered her out of sight to any passer-by.

'Hello,' she said with a doubtful smile.

'Oh Wendy! You *have* been a naughty girl. We've been searching for you for ages. Dr Crosland!' Bryony called to his receding back. Then again, 'Dr Crosland!'

He was some way away but it was quiet on the beach and he paused for a moment, listening, then turned and saw them.

Bryony beckoned to him. As he neared them she was dismayed at the pallor of his face and the lines which appeared to have been newly-etched on it. His yellow eyes were blazing.

'Wendy! What is the meaning of this? Why did you run away?'

She raised her small pixie-like face. 'I wanted to.'

'Do you realise that you have disrupted the work at the hospital? And caused a great deal of trouble to a number of people?'

'I guess so,' she said, giving him a sidelong glance.

'Why did you run away?' he demanded sternly.

She twisted her heel to and fro with a squeaking sound and made no reply.

'Wendy!' His voice was quiet but nevertheless Bryony's heart leapt. 'I have asked you a question. Answer me, please.'

'I forgot what you asked me,' she said.

'Why did you run away?'

She tossed her pony-tail from side to side deliberately. 'Like I said, because I wanted to.'

The corners of his mouth tightened. 'You are never to do such a thing again, do you understand?'

'I shall though.' Her eyes were bright and challenging.

'I said no,' Ellis warned her, with controlled anger.

She looked down at her shoes. 'I probably will though,' she said defiantly.

With one swift movement he lifted her, put her across his knee and spanked her. She burst into noisy sobs and rolled over on to her face on the pebbles.

'Stay there until I say you may get up,' he said firmly.

He gripped Bryony's arm and led her down to the water's edge. Her heart was thudding.

'She's only a child,' she said accusingly.

'I don't need you to tell me her age,' he replied stiffly.

'But you hurt her!'

He looked down at her quizzically. 'Do you really believe that?'

'Of course I do. You don't realise how much bigger and stronger you are.'

'A slapped bottom never did any naughty child any harm. The only thing that is hurt is her dignity, and she has to learn what she can and cannot do. What would you like me to have done? Bought her a lollipop and told her that we quite understood and she wasn't really naughty? I have no patience with that school of thought.'

'I have always heard it said that you shouldn't punish anyone when you are angry. You could hurt them more than you realise,' Bryony protested.

'To that I say rubbish. I think it is quite barbaric

to threaten someone with punishment and for them to have the fear of it hanging over them and then to beat them in cold blood. No. Wendy was very naughty and had to be punished now. In that way she will connect the two and hopefully that will make her consider twice before she repeats the misdeed.'

Bryony stood stiffly and silently beside him. He slipped his arm around her waist. 'I have her welfare at heart, you know,' he said softly. 'Her father would not thank me if I allowed her to misbehave and didn't chastise her.' Then with a stern note in his voice he added, 'Quite apart from that she has caused us all a great deal of worry and inconvenience, and she deserved to be beaten. I think she got off very lightly.'

Bryony shivered and his arm tightened around her. She hoped that she would never incur his anger for she firmly believed that he was no respecter of persons and would mete out similar punishment to anybody if he considered that they deserved it.

'I wonder why she ran way?' she said.

'I shall have to find out, but she can be very obstinate.' He sighed. 'It is a great responsibility having to care for her on my own. Her parents trust me implicitly, I couldn't let them down.'

'Despite what she said I doubt if she would run away again,' Bryony said, to comfort him.

He looked at her with warmth in his eyes and she felt a tremendous relief that the anxiety had disappeared.

'I haven't thanked you for giving up your time to help me, Bryony. I am very grateful.'

They walked back to where Wendy was lying silently now.

'Wendy?' Ellis's voice was gentle. 'You may get up now.'

She scrambled to her feet looking dishevelled with her crumpled dress and tear-stained face.

'Have you anything you wish to say?' he asked.

'Sorry, Uncle Ellis,' she muttered.

He took her small chin in his hand and tilted up her face. 'Are we friends?'

With a sudden movement she flung herself against him and wrapped her arms around his thighs. 'I love you, Uncle Ellis,' she said brokenly.

'And I love you.' He lifted her up off the ground and kissed her.

She giggled and struggled and tugged his hair.

'Oh, it's rough stuff, is it?' he laughed, and swung her high in the air before setting her down on her feet.

She clung to his hand. 'You do love me, don't you, Uncle Ellis?'

He bent down and looked into her face. 'You know that I do. That is why I spanked you. I want you to become a nice young lady not a spoilt brat. Now that we have cleared that up, tell me why you ran away.'

Wendy scowled down at the pebbles. 'Because I don't like her.'

'You don't like who?'

'Dr Browne. I don't like her one little bit. And if you marry her I shall run away for ever and ever.' Then, remembering, she covered her bottom with both hands and looked up at him apprehensively.

'If I do *what*?' he asked in astonishment.

'If you marry her,' Wendy repeated.

'What on earth makes you think I would do that?'

Bryony was so still during this interchange that she could have been made of stone.

'Because she said so.'

Ellis frowned. 'She? Please give the lady her name.'

'You know her name,' Wendy pouted.

'Wendy!' He said warningly.

'Dr Browne,' she muttered hastily.

'Tell me exactly what she said, please, because I think you misunderstood her.'

'No I didn't either. She said that when you married her I would be at boarding school, that's what she said.'

Ellis studied her thoughtfully. 'And what had you said or done to provoke that remark?' he demanded.

Wendy gave him a guilty sidelong glance. Then, obviously thinking that her reply might make her unpopular with him, she moved over to Bryony and stood on the far side.

'I—said—I didn't—much—like being with her.'

Bryony glanced at Ellis and saw the corners of his mouth twitch.

'That was not a very polite thing to say, was it? When she was so kind as to let you stay there with her?' he suggested.

'Well you've said I must always tell the truth and that was the truth. I don't like being with her. And I don't like going on picnics with her either and going into horrid old hotels. And both of you talking to each other and not taking any notice of me at all. I don't think that is very polite either.'

'Well I hope you didn't tell her all that,' Ellis said, a glimmer of amusement in his eyes.

'I did though,' she said happily. 'That's when she said she didn't like me going on picnics with her and you either, and that soon I'd be out of the way at boarding-school. And she said, "Thank goodness you'll be out of the way when we get married".'

Ellis wrinkled up his forehead. 'This is all very embarrassing, I hardly know what to do about it.'

'Oh it's all right, Uncle Ellis. I told her you weren't going to marry her because you were going to marry Nurse Sellers.'

The colour rushed to Bryony's cheeks and her heart raced. She would have given a great deal to have been standing on quicksand so that she could have sunk out of sight.

'She didn't like that a bit,' Wendy confided contentedly.

'And I don't like it a bit either,' Ellis said angrily. 'You had absolutely no business to say that, and running away afterwards certainly did nothing to put it right.'

'I know it wasn't telling the truth but I'm glad I said it all the same.'

'And now I hope you are going to enjoy telling Dr Browne that you were not speaking the truth and that you are sorry,' he said.

Wendy slipped her hand in Bryony's. 'If you marry Nurse Sellers that will make it true and then I won't have to.'

Horror and dismay coursed through Bryony like twin flames. She spoke quickly to cover her embarrassment.

'Hold on, Wendy,' she said, trying to laugh. 'I shall be leaving here soon, I've got other plans.'

'You're going away?' Wendy looked at her with disappointed eyes.

'You're going away?' Ellis's voice was hard and questioning.

Bryony swallowed and passed the tip of her tongue over her suddenly dry lips. 'Yes,' she said.

'But I don't want you to go,' Wendy cried.

'When you go to school and when your parents come home you will soon forget all about me,' Bryony said.

'Why are you going away?' Wendy whined.

'Where are you going?' Ellis asked.

Bryony looked from one to the other of them and caught her breath.

'A patient at Highfields—Mrs Trengwainton—has asked me to go and live with her as her private nurse,' she said. And immediately felt desolate.

Wendy opened her mouth to protest further but Ellis silenced her.

'This is neither the time nor the place for such a discussion.' He turned to Bryony. 'I will see you in my rooms tomorrow at four o'clock, if you please.'

'Very well, sir.' Bryony looked at his unfathomable topaz eyes with a feeling of heartbreak. She had to get away from him this minute or she would shame everybody by bursting into tears. With a sharp intake of breath she continued,

'If you don't mind I would like to walk home now.'

'We are just leaving. I will give you a lift,' he said.

'No thank you, I fancy the walk.'

She ran her hand affectionately over Wendy's head, then ran up the beach, up the steps, and across to the esplanade.

CHAPTER TEN

ONLY when Bryony reached the esplanade did she stop running. There was no fear, now, of Ellis catching up with her for his car was parked at the far end. She wanted to be alone for a while so she went into a small café. She was the only customer, for it was late for afternoon tea and early for evening coffee. She bought a cup of tea at the counter and took it to a plastic-topped table by the window.

The sun had almost set. Soon lights would spring up in the streets and houses and it would be brighter. Now everywhere seemed grey and sombre. She was immensely relieved that Wendy had been found. For her to have been missing when night fell would have been horrific, no wonder Ellis had been so worried and angry, but it was anger born of love as he had later shown. She envied Wendy for the love and anger he had bestowed on her, it proved that he had a depth of feeling for her which she herself longed for in vain.

She wondered if she could ever forget Wendy's embarrassing suggestion and the way in which Ellis had dismissed it, but the words were as loud and clear in her head as if someone was here in the café shouting them for all the world to hear. She could not feel comforted by the fact that Ellis put on a show of being surprised that Thea Browne had declared that they were to be married. Naturally he would deny it for that was not the way either of them would choose to make the announcement. Bryony was secretly pleased that Wendy had told Thea that Ellis was going to marry herself, even though it was not true. She had a feeling of glee when she pictured the scene. Dr Browne would have been furious! She was known to have a temper as fiery as her hair, so no wonder Wendy had run away.

The pleasure only lasted a minute. One thing had led to another and it was because of it that Bryony had said she was going to work for Mrs Trengwainton and now that she had committed herself she was more than ever riddled with doubts. She seemed to hear that monotonous voice as she complained of one thing or another. She was well aware that she would have to pander to her every whim and would be made to feel she was an inferior being. Forfeiting her pride in her chosen profession would be the high price she would pay for a life of luxury. A life of loneliness, too, for there would be no young people for company.

She pushed her tea aside, untasted, and got to her feet. She was late for her evening meal and would probably have to eat alone. There would be no one to take her mind off her problems.

As she passed Highfields she felt an unexpected affection for it. It was not bright and homely and exciting like St Stephen's, but she was beginning to feel she was a part of it. She looked sadly at Dr Crosland's house and an ache of longing gripped her heart. When she went away she would never again see Wendy looking out of the window or Ellis striding down the path. She gave herself a mental shake. Wasn't it because of him that she was wanting to get away? Because of the torture of seeing him and loving him and knowing that she could never hope to be more to him than an unimportant nurse who sometimes accompanied him and Wendy on outings? For even if he had no intention of marrying Dr Browne he was even less likely to marry herself, no matter what Wendy suggested, for she had nothing to offer him that he would value, neither money nor status nor influential relations. It was imperative that she went away. But to Mrs Trengwainton?

She heard a car approaching and then it stopped. Bryony's heart missed a beat as she saw Ellis and Wendy walk hand-in-hand up the path and into his house. How was it possible for him to look more attractive each time she saw him?

She walked slowly up the steps of Harbour View. As she opened the door Mrs Rosewall hurried to meet her.

'I'm sorry I'm late, something important cropped up and I was unable to let you know, Mrs Rosewall. I do hope I didn't put you out.'

Mrs Rosewall brushed the apology aside, her face was full of excitement. 'That's all right, I've put your supper in the oven to keep hot, but don't leave it there too long. You've got a visitor, Nurse. He's waiting for you in the living-room and we're having our coffee in the dining-room so that you won't be disturbed.'

'A visitor?' Bryony's thoughts flew anxiously to her parents and she hoped that nothing was wrong. 'Thank you, Mrs Rosewall.'

She opened the door curiously and came face to face with the last person she expected to see. Momentarily the room and everything in it seemed to spin around anti-clockwise and propel her backwards in time. The young man who rose to meet her had not changed at all. And yet in that first split second he seemed to look almost effeminate. Had his hair always been so fair and wavy? His complexion so pink and white? His body so slight? She blinked and he was none of those things, he had only appeared to be in contrast to the man who had been occupying her thoughts.

'Hello Bryony,' he said, a doubtful smile on his face.

'Nick!' That was all she could say.

'It is good to see you.' He took a step towards her but she moved back.

'Why have you come here?'

'Because I wanted to see you, Bryony, it's as simple as that,' he said with the humorous expression in his eyes that used to so attract her.

She felt indignant at his easy manner. 'I can't imagine why.'

'I want to talk to you,' he said, the smile going from his eyes.

She turned her head aside. 'I don't think we have anything to say to one another.'

'Please Bryony!' His voice was gently persuasive. 'I want to talk to you, but not like this. Please sit down.' He pushed a chair towards her.

She sat on the edge of it reluctantly and waited for him to speak.

'Your mother gave me your address,' he said.

'Mother did? Why? What did you say to her?'

'That I wanted to see you. She seemed pleased.'

Mother would have been, Bryony thought. Her parents had been fond of Nick, had thought of him as a son, and Bryony knew that they believed that she had been most to blame for the break-up. It was her own pride that had made her encourage them in that belief, for to be jilted was so shaming. She believed that she would never fully recover from it.

'How were my parents?' she asked.

'They both looked very well, but they miss you. I miss you, too.'

Bryony looked at him coldly. 'Is your wife with you?'

He shook his head. 'I'm not married, Bryony.'

She felt a jolt of surprise. 'I'm sorry, I thought you were. So is your fiancée with you?' She spoke politely as if speaking to a casual acquaintance instead of the man who had been the most important person in her life at one time.

'I haven't got one,' he said.

'Another broken engagement? These things usually happen in threes. So who is the luckless girl who is next in line?' Her voice was bitter.

He moved uncomfortably. 'Don't be like that, Bryony, you were always such a sweet girl.'

'And look where that got me! Anyhow, people change. I found that out too, some time ago.'

'I'm sorry, I really am. But that is what I've come here to speak to you about.' He started to walk towards her, but on seeing the expression on her face he stopped.

'Well here I am. What did you want to say to me?'

He looked around the room with a helpless gesture. 'How can I speak to you like this?'

She stood up. 'We can't keep the family out of this room any longer, they sit in here in the evenings to watch television. And I haven't had my meal yet. I don't really think we have anything important to discuss, so—' She shrugged.

He laid his hand tentatively on her arm. 'Bryony—please don't send me away without at least hearing what I have to say. Can I meet you somewhere later this evening?'

She glanced at the clock on the mantelpiece. Mrs Rosewall would be missing her favourite programme if Nick did not leave now.

'Very well. I'll meet you at the end of this road where it joins the esplanade in an hour's time.'

'Thank you, Bryony. I'll be there.'

When the front door closed after him Mrs Rosewall popped out of the dining-room like a jack-in-the-box. She seemed more interested in Nick than in her programme. Her brown eyes sparkled with curiosity.

'What a good-looking young man, Nurse, and so pleasant. I was speaking to him before you came in. Is he someone special?'

Special? Of course he was special, he had been a part of her life.

'No,' she said bleakly, 'nobody special, just someone I used to know.'

'Well he's come a long way to see you again by all accounts,' she said with a wink. 'He must be keen on you.'

Bryony gave a little unamused laugh. 'I don't think so.'

She took her meal from the oven. It was steak pie, runner beans and potatoes but she tasted nothing. So Nick had come back to her. Was it Fate that had sent him in time to save her from going to Mrs Trengwainton? That could solve her problem. Possibly she was suffering from the shock of seeing him so unexpectedly, but although she had loved him so much and had endured such misery when he jilted her, she could feel nothing for him at all. She was neither sorry nor glad that he had come to her, she felt like a scientist studying an insect under a microscope, interested but not emotionally involved. She tried to recapture the love she had felt for him, to remember the sheer joy of being with him, but in vain.

When she had finished eating the sherry trifle which Mrs Rosewall had made with such care she took the dishes to the kitchen and washed them. Then she went upstairs to change. Something feminine inside her shamed her by making her want to look her best. She looked critically at the clothes hanging in her wardrobe and chose a periwinkle-blue suit in a loose-woven woollen material. Blue was Nick's favourite colour and this was to have been her going-away outfit. She fastened a choker of silver and rough-cut blue stones around her neck, and after studying herself in the mirror, put more colour than usual on her pale cheeks. She tilted her chin and tossed the fair hair from her face. Then she went downstairs.

Mrs Rosewall popped her head around the door. 'Oh my! You do look a picture! Janice, come and see.'

Bryony laughed in embarrassment at their admiring eyes.

'I think you must be going to meet that young man,' Mrs Rosewall said knowingly. 'And a lovely-looking couple you make.'

With those encouraging words ringing in her ears Bryony walked down the road. She was deeply grateful for their praise. Nick had jilted her. Maybe he had come here expecting to find her looking miserable and uninterested in her appearance. Instead, she was someone whom he might regret losing, for appearance had always mattered to him.

He was standing where they had arranged to

meet. In the past how her heart had rejoiced whenever she had seen him. Tonight there was no joy, no delight at all.

He held out both hands as she drew near. On his face was the look of someone who has seen a rainbow for the first time and is enchanted by it.

'Bryony! Oh Bryony, you look beautiful,' he said.

'Thank you,' she said coolly. 'You had something to say to me?'

There was no doubt about it, he was good-looking. His fair hair was thick and springy and she had a sudden memory of how she used to like to run her fingers through it. In the past his very blue eyes had always been smiling but tonight they were serious. This was the man whom she had loved and lost and who had caused her not only grief but disillusionment and it was that which made her distrust the motives of every man.

'Is there somewhere we can go to sit?' he asked.

'There is an inn near the harbour. We can go there if you like.'

It was early, so it was not crowded, and they were able to find a table well away from the bar.

'The usual?' Nick asked.

It was that touch of remembered familiarity which suddenly awoke Bryony's emotions. Her eyes pricked with unexpected tears. Oh Nick, Nick, her heart cried, why did it all go wrong?

She nodded silently. He came back with the drinks and sat beside her.

'To us,' he said.

Bryony took a sip of her wine to steady her trembling lips.

'First of all I owe you an apology,' Nick said.

Indignation made her snap, 'An apology!'

'I know that is not enough, but what more can I say? Do you want me to go down on my bended?' His eyes crinkled in the old way as they smiled at her. 'I will do that, if you insist.'

She shook her head and said coldly, 'No, you don't have to do or say anything. What's done is done and nothing can wipe it out.'

'Not even though I have come back to you because I love you?'

'No. As I see it, you decided very late in the day that you didn't want to marry me because you met someone you liked better. However, for some reason that hasn't worked out so now you've come back hoping to carry on where we left off. Am I right?'

'Put that way it sounds awful.'

'I agree. So let me hear how you put it.'

He lit a cigarette. He had not smoked in the past.

'I loved you very much, Bryony, and we got on famously, you must admit.'

'I never denied it.'

He drew on his cigarette. 'It was because I loved you so much that I found myself worrying about the future—financially, I mean. I earned so little from my cartoons but I wasn't qualified to do anything else. And it was the only work I wanted to do.'

'I knew that, Nick, we both knew it all along and we had discussed it,' Bryony said, remembering his amusing, exaggerated drawings of what life would be like for them living on the bread-line.

'Yes, I could laugh about it when we were together. It was when I was alone that I realised that I would mostly be living on your earnings, and that you worked a darned sight harder than I ever did. I didn't like that thought.'

Bryony was silent for a few minutes. 'I can understand that, Nick. But what I can't understand is why you left it so late before you decided that you couldn't go through with it. Didn't you for one moment consider what it would be like for me? For my family? They had booked the hotel and invited the guests—my wedding dress and the bridesmaids' dresses were made—' She choked on those words, as she remembered the embarrassment and the shame of cancelling the arrangements, informing the guests. And most of all the heartbreak of losing Nick which she could not mention.

He stubbed out his cigarette and ground it into the ashtray.

'Because I was a coward. I kept trying to say something to you and then putting it off. Those last few weeks you must have guessed that something was wrong. I couldn't pretend any more.'

'And it coincided with your meeting Pamela Cutts, didn't it?' she said bitterly. 'A father-in-law in the publishing world was the answer to your problem, wasn't it?'

He absent-mindedly took another cigarette. 'That was true. It seemed a wonderful stroke of luck when I met the Cutts, but not for the reason you seem to imagine. I thought that if I could become really friendly with them I might sell more cartoons and it would be better for you and me. I honestly didn't think that Pam would be interested in an unsuccessful cartoonist like me. But apparently she was and things just took off from there,' he said miserably.

Bryony looked at him with disgust. 'So you broke our engagement although you didn't fall in love with her? I think that makes it worse.'

Nick frowned. 'You've got it all wrong. I don't mean that at all. I'm saying that is how it started. Eventually I thought I loved her—for all kinds of reasons.'

'So what went wrong?'

He shook his head. 'Nothing in particular—but everything.'

'I don't know what that means.'

'I suppose I had too good an opinion of myself. I thought my work was good and it only needed a word from someone at the top to an editor for me to get a regular commission. I was wrong. The fact is that my work is not good enough.'

'Oh it is,' Bryony protested. 'Some of your cartoons were excellent.'

'Some of them, yes, but some of them aren't, and to make a proper living they need to be good all of the time and no amount of influence is going to get an editor to buy them if they are not.'

'Don't tell me that you broke your engagement to Pamela Cutts because her father couldn't help you after all!'

He gave a short, mirthless laugh. 'I suppose in a way it is a compliment that you think it was I who broke it off.'

'Wasn't it? You'd had practise.'

'Pamela met a wealthy businessman, and that was that.'

'She broke it off?'

'It was more or less mutual. At the same time that she met him I realised that if I were to marry her without being successful I would be back to square one, living on her, as I would have been on you.'

Bryony studied his good-looking face and for the first time noticed the weakness in his mouth and chin. How shallow his love had been for both her and Pamela, despite his excuses. The trouble all around was money, the desire for more money. First him, then Pamela. And Ellis, too. Of course you needed money to live, but how sordid and unromantic was the search for it.

'So what are you doing now?' she asked.

'Doing?'

'Are you still doing cartoons?'

'Yes. As I told you there is nothing else I can do.'

She felt sad at his lack of success and bleak outlook.

'You haven't told me yet why you wanted to see me.'

'I've told you one of the reasons. I wanted you to know why I did what I did. At the time we couldn't discuss it because you wouldn't see me and I can't pretend that I wasn't relieved. It would have been very painful.'

Painful? Of course it was painful, it was agonising, a voice inside her screamed.

'I see. And the other reasons?'

'You may find this difficult to believe, but hardly a day passes when I don't think of you. As time went on I missed the fun we had, the happiness—'

'Thank you for telling me that. It was the shared laughter that I missed most,' she admitted.

He smiled eagerly, remembering. 'I would always rather show my cartoons to you than anyone else, we have the same sense of humour.'

'We did have.'

He leaned towards her and took her hand. 'We could have it all again, Bryony, we are both free. At least—' A shadow crossed his face. 'I presume you are free?'

'I'm not engaged, if that's what you mean.'

'Then come back to London, let's start again and share the fun we had. Will you, Bryony?'

She looked at him in surprise. 'So you wouldn't mind living on my earnings now?'

'I don't mean get married,' he said hastily. 'Not yet anyway, not until I'm more successful. We could share a flat and each pay our own way. Lots of couples do that and make a success of it.'

She twisted her glass in her hands. She thought of her immediate future. There was Mrs Trengwainton's offer, or Nick's. She tried to picture what it would be like with Nick. Would she be able to recapture that feeling of love she once had for him? Could they be happy? He had given a feasible explanation for what he had done and had come back to her. Surely she was not so bitter that she could never forgive him? No, it was not bitterness which would make her refuse his suggestion but the fact that she no longer loved him. It was Ellis Crosland who had all her love and who had won her heart. Unfortunately it was a trophy he did not want, like winning a goldfish at a fair when you had nowhere to put it and didn't like it anyway.

'Bryony?'

With a start she realised that he had spoken to her.

'I'm sorry, Nick, I was thinking over what you said. But it would be no good. Everything has changed. I know it was not so very long ago but I feel a different person now. It taught me something and now I see people and life in another way. That love we shared, and the fun, it's gone, Nick, and we could never get it back. It would be foolish even to try.'

He thumped the table with his fist. 'Oh what a mess I've made of everything. It was such a good thing we had going.' He took her hand and squeezed it hard.

'But we can't turn the clock back, Nick. Thank you for coming to see me, I appreciate that. And I wish you every success. I'll look out for your cartoons.' She stood up.

'Please Bryony, don't turn me down. I know this must have come as a surprise to you. Don't answer me now. Please think about it some more.'

She wanted to leave, wanted to be able to think of what they had lost, of what might have been, without being shamed, her resolve shaken by tears.

She laid her hand on his arm briefly. 'I'm sorry, Nick. Goodbye,' she said sadly, then went out into the night.

CHAPTER ELEVEN

FOUR O'CLOCK loomed menacingly ahead. The thought of the interview with Ellis scared Bryony. She saw no reason for the meeting for there was nothing to discuss. She had made her decision and what she had decided was up to her, wasn't it? Or was it? Had she perhaps not read the small print in her contract which said she could not leave until after a certain specified length of time?

There were two new admissions during the morning. One was seven-month-old Jason Cornish, the only child of the Mayor and Mayoress of Polwithy. He had been born to them when they had feared they would be childless and so was particularly precious. The baby was suffering from gastro-enteritis and was severely dehydrated. He was put in the exclusive care of Staff Nurse Bennet.

The other was a middle-aged, highly successful but overworked estate agent. Tests were being run to find the cause of his headaches and attacks of giddiness.

These admissions meant that all the bedrooms were now occupied so it was probable that Mrs Trengwainton would be discharged and Bryony's time of decision was fast coming to an end.

'Rene,' she said to Nurse Dyson when they were

at lunch. 'Do you know if there is any rule which says we can't leave here until we've been here for a certain length of time?'

Rene was eating her poached trout and creamed potatoes with obvious enjoyment. 'Not that I know of. And the answer doesn't interest me. As long as they feed me food like this I'll never ask to leave. The only way they can get rid of me will be to chuck me out. Why do you ask?'

'I—I just wondered, that's all. Where could I find out?'

'Goodness knows. Sister Mailer, I should think. But if you want my opinion for what it's worth I'd say that if someone wanted to leave they couldn't stop them.'

'Not even if it said something else in the contract?'

'Not even then. How do you suppose they'd stop you? By taking you to court?'

Bryony looked dubious. 'Well yes, I suppose they could do that.'

'And get it reported in the local rag? "Nurse sued for wanting to leave nursing home for the wealthy. What are the reasons behind this? Should the running of the home be investigated?" Do you think they would risk getting that sort of publicity?' Rene said with a laugh and started on her lemon cream pie.

Strangely, Bryony felt no relief at hearing Rene's opinion. So Dr Crosland would not be forbidding her to leave but probably suggesting that she and

Mrs Trengwainton should leave at the same time. She looked bleakly into space.

'So what's biting you?' Rene asked, looking to see where the cheeseboard was.

Bryony mentally shook herself. 'Nothing in particular. Do you know whether a date has been fixed for Mrs Trengwainton to leave?'

'Not that I know of, though I can't imagine why. She's as fit as a flea and just as jumpy. Every time I go into her room she looks up to see if it's you and when she sees it isn't she gives me that "What on earth are you doing in a place like this" look. I'm getting fed up with her, you'll have to start seeing her again soon. Unless she leaves.'

Bryony nodded. 'Yes, I know I will. But thanks a lot for doing it for me, I'm really grateful.'

'Actually if you close your ears to her monotonous voice she isn't a bad old stick. She's very generous, I'll say that for her.'

'Yes, I know she is. But I get tired of hearing her going on about her symptoms, too,' Bryony sighed.

'You know I'd do anything for anyone who is ill, it really gives me a thrill to help in any way I can, I don't care if they're old or young or men or women, I just love doing it. But what I can't stand is running around after someone who is as well as I am myself. And I can't believe there is anything the matter with Mrs Trengwainton and I don't mean that unkindly.' Rene cut herself a massive wedge of cheese and helped herself liberally to biscuits and butter.

'She's a good source of income to Highfields,' Bryony murmured.

'That's true enough.' A shower of crumbs fell around Rene's plate. 'But the beds are always in demand. I shouldn't have thought they would keep anyone in here unnecessarily.

'But a patient who is already in bed is worth two who might or might not take their place,' Bryony said.

Rene wrinkled up her nose. 'You talking about them sharing?'

Bryony laughed. 'No, I was thinking that a bird in the hand is worth two in the bush, but it didn't come out right. Well, I don't worry about Mrs Trengwainton being kept here because she can well afford it but I feel sorry for little Mrs Boase, the one with the ulcer. Her husband is not at all well off, she told me.'

'Mrs Boase? I haven't had anything to do with her. It's you and Nurse Patel, isn't it? But take it from me, one thing is certain. What you or I think makes no difference. Our lord and master, Dr Crosland, is one of the "I'll do it my way" brigade. That could be his signature tune.'

'That's true enough. You never hear anything about his partner, do you? I've never seen him to my knowledge, have you?'

'No, he's just a sleeping-partner. Could be a woman, I suppose. Perhaps it's Dr Browne, who knows? Anyhow it makes no difference. The Boss-man is Dr Crosland, and very dishy he is too.'

'Ho, ho! I thought you knew your place in life and had your own fella and all that?' Bryony teased.

'I do and I have. And jolly glad I am too. Because if I didn't, I might—just *might* be a silly slob and fall in love with him. I can imagine those manly arms around me clutching me to his manly bosom—or is it chest? Those yellow eyes looking into mine and that cruel mouth—'

Bryony pushed her chair back abruptly. 'Sorry, I can't stay to hear the rest of your revolting romance, I've got to get back.'

Not for another moment could she have stayed there to hear a mockery being made of her inner feelings. Maybe if she could have laughed with Rene it would have helped, but that was impossible. She had not finished her meal and she had another quarter of an hour before she was due back on duty but she wanted to be alone.

She went out into the garden and sat in a deckchair which had been put there for a patient who was now at lunch. It was a perfect summer day and not too hot in the garden because of the light breeze which blew in from the sea. The flower beds were a riot of colour with dahlias and chrysanthemums and fuchsias bordering the lawns which sloped down towards the sea. A trellis covered with sweet smelling honeysuckle provided a shelter from the wind when it blew from the south-west. Ahead was the bay which shone in silver ripples against the white heat of the sky, surrounded by long fingers of green fields and dark cliffs. Standing sentinel, a pyramid of foliage capped by a fairytale castle, was the Mount. On the esplanade, holidaymakers lounged in deck-chairs, while elderly residents occupied the shelters. On the road, cars took children and toddlers to sandier beaches or drove to famous beauty spots. Polwithy was a holiday resort without many amusements and for that reason had a charm all of its own.

Bryony breathed in the salty air contentedly. Anyone who could afford to pay the exorbitant fees here should be happy. The food was excellent as also was the attention. And as a bonus there were these beautiful surroundings.

With a catch at her heart she saw Ellis drive past the bottom of the garden and park outside his house next door. Today was his day for seeing private patients. In three hours' time she would be going there for her interview. Would she be sandwiched between patients? Or be the last on his list?

The town clock struck an unmusical hour. She stood up, smoothed down her dress and walked slowly back indoors to do the familiar round of patients again. Today it seemed boring and she believed that she preferred working in A and E, there was an exciting urgency about the department. You could be dealing with street accident victims, fractured limbs, foreign bodies in an eye, splinters, cuts and bruises, and your patients would be of any age or sex. Even in a surgical ward you had the drama of pre and post-operative cases which broke the monotony. But here the atmosphere was like visiting elderly relatives on a Sunday afternoon.

She passed Mrs Trengwainton's door with a feeling of guilt and went on to visit Winston Deansborough. He stood up without the aid of his crutch when she entered the room.

'Well done, Mr Deansborough, that's splendid, isn't it? How does your leg feel? Is it quite better?'

He gave her a beaming smile. The pallor had gone from his face and his teeth gleamed even whiter than usual.

'It is as good as new. I am very fine indeed, thank you. You are most kind.'

His pulse rate, temperature and blood pressure were all satisfactory.

'So I suppose you will be leaving us,' Bryony said.

He held up his hand, pink palm towards her. 'Ah, no! My leg it is all right, but tests are being made of my blood to make quite sure I am recovered. It is good to be careful, Dr Crosland say.'

'Yes of course,' she said. But she thought bitterly that another week or so would all help to make Dr Crosland into a millionaire which was apparently what he wanted.

She went next to Mrs Boase who was sitting in a chair by the open french door.

'You are in a lovely spot there, but it would do you good to be out in the garden, we don't get many days like this,' Bryony said.

Rosemary smiled up at her. 'I'd rather be here, not having to talk to any of the other patients. It's so lovely, like being in a five star hotel—although I've never tried that. But this is something I'll remember all my life, especially as I am feeling so much better than I have for years.'

'Good, that's splendid. And no talk of surgery?'

'No, Dr Crosland hasn't mentioned it.'

As Bryony unwrapped the cuff of the sphygmomanometer she wondered what Rosemary had done about moving to Polwithy.

'Have you spoken to Sister Mailer about it?' she asked.

A look of warm happiness spread over the young woman's face. 'Well, no. I mentioned it to Brian and said what I intended to do but he said it was worth paying anything for me to get really well. So he's taken out another mortgage on our house. It just means we'll go on paying for a few extra years. But we hope to be able to pay it off sooner than that.'

Bryony was both touched and appalled. 'You lucky girl, you must have a super husband. But is it worth it? Polwithy is an excellent hospital, you know.'

'Oh yes,' Rosemary said hastily. 'We've got nothing against it at all. But it's Dr Crosland, you see. I want to be his private patient, he has been so wonderfully good and kind.'

'He has patients in Polwithy too,' Bryony said

gently, wondering why she was pursuing the subject.

'Yes I know that, but it wouldn't be the same. He couldn't possibly give me the attention there that he does here. And—I know you'll think I'm being silly—but I believe just seeing him does me more good than even the medicine he has prescribed.'

Bryony took a good look at her. Now that her mind was at rest and the anxious expression had gone she was a pretty girl. Just another on a list of pretty girls who had fallen for Ellis over the years.

When it was nearly four o'clock she went to the changing-room, took off her uniform and changed into the light grey dress which Janice had so admired. The large white collar and trimmings were immaculate and flattering and the belt accentuated her tiny waist. Her fair hair had recently been trimmed and was brushed back at the sides so that her white ear-rings were visible. Satisfied with her appearance she set off for the house next door. This would be the first time she had been inside his house. She walked up the flight of steps, took several very deep breaths, then, as the front door was open, went into the spacious hall, which had a large, beautifully coloured persian carpet on a polished wood floor.

The middle-aged pleasant receptionist behind a mellow walnut desk greeted her with a smile.

'I am so sorry, do please forgive me, but I don't seem to have you down.' She was searching through the appointments book. 'Is Dr Crosland expecting you?'

'Yes, my appointment is for four o'clock. My name is Sellers.'

The receptionist picked up the telephone. 'There is a Miss Sellers for you, Doctor. I haven't got a—oh, I see. Thank you.'

She replaced the receiver. 'Will you go through, please Miss Sellers?'

Bryony opened the door nervously. Her first impression of the room was that it was enormous. Next, that it was elegantly and expensively furnished. There were cream suede settees and armchairs, full length cream and scarlet brocade curtains, scarlet scatter cushions and bowls of roses of all colours. Behind a massive mahogany desk which was the predominating feature of the room, sat Ellis. He wore a perfectly-tailored light grey hand-stitched suit, and an eye-catching brown and gold silk tie on his white shirt. There were a few silvery strands in his crisp, chestnut hair, at the temples, which gave him a distinguished air. There was an absent-minded look in his eyes as he glanced up at her.

'Good afternoon, Nurse, do please take a seat. I won't keep you a minute.'

She believed it was a deliberate ploy that the chair was so low that anyone sitting on it had to look up at him. She watched in fascination as he read a paper, then signed it with a slim gold pen. He folded it, put it in an envelope which he addressed and placed on a silver tray beside him. His fingers were long and tapered and well-manicured. From beneath his shirt cuff there was the glint of gold from an oval watch, and the tips of the brown hairs on his wrist. Her eyes travelled up to the firm, well-shaped mouth and square jaw, and it was clear that his word would be law. When he suddenly spoke he startled her.

'Yes, Nurse. What was it you wanted to see me about?'

His eyes were brilliantly yellow as they gazed down at her and his mouth was curved invitingly. His voice was gentle and interested. This, she decided, was his 'private patient' approach.

She ran her tongue across her lips. 'Nothing. It was you who asked me to come here, sir.'

His eyebrows puckered momentarily as he studied her very deliberately, seeming to notice everything about her, even the details of her dress.

'I did?' There was quizzical enquiry in his eyes. 'I'm sorry. Would you put me in the picture?'

So this interview which had caused her so many hours of worry had entirely skipped his mind. How foolish she had been to imagine that he would have been thinking of it too.

'I think you wanted me to hand in my notice to you personally,' she said abruptly.

The quizzical gleam died out of his eyes. 'I wanted you to do what?' he asked irritably.

'I mentioned that I was leaving to work for Mrs Trengwainton and you said we should discuss it today,' she said, speaking as irritably as he had.

A look of awareness came into his eyes. 'Oh yes, of course. That was yesterday when we were all somewhat upset. I think you said what you did on the spur of the moment, so we will forget it.' He gave her a charming smile, his eyes crinkled, his mouth turned down, almost as if he was laughing at her. 'Was there anything else you wished to say to me?'

She felt a blaze of annoyance that he should dismiss the subject so casually.

'I know that we were all upset yesterday but that merely precipitated my intention of leaving. I should be glad if you would accept my notice. How long should it be? A week or a month?' Her grey eyes, dark now, looked angrily into his.

He threw back his head and laughed as if he was genuinely amused.

'Come now, Nurse, you are not going to let your embarrassment at a childish remark force you to such extreme lengths, surely?'

So he *did* remember! The colour flooded her cheeks. 'It was nothing to do with that. I was going to tell you anyway, only . . . well, it was because of what Wendy said that I told you at that moment.'

He studied her silently for a minute or so. 'And what on earth do you imagine you would be doing at Mrs Trengwainton's home? Looking after her chihuahuas? I understand she has several,' he said derisively.

'No, sir, I would be her nurse,' Bryony snapped.

'Her nurse? She doesn't need a nurse, you must realise that.'

'She believes that she does. And she wants me. She has offered to double my salary and give me a car.' She looked at him challengingly.

He pushed his chair back and rising slowly to his feet walked around his desk and stood in front of her. He surveyed her from under frowning brows.

'So you are prepared to give up your career to bury yourself at the back of beyond and live with an elderly woman who does not require your skills? For the sake of the money she would pay you? You mean to tell me that you can be bought?' His eyes met and held hers for a moment. 'You disappoint me,' he said coldly.

How dared he attribute his faults to herself! 'If there is nothing wrong with Mrs Trengwainton, then why has she been at Highfields for so long? Why are you still keeping her there?'

He took a step closer to her and something inside her trembled.

'Are you presuming to question my line of treatment, Nurse? Have I been misinformed? Are you a doctor qualified to ask me such a thing?' His mouth twisted sardonically.

'No, of course not, and you know that,' she murmured. Then, on seeing what she took to be a look of smug satisfaction on his face, she added with all the bitterness that had been building up inside her ever since Nick had jilted her, 'But I *am* a nurse and I've got eyes in my head. I don't think there is anything wrong with Mrs Trengwainton and you have just assured me there isn't. So naturally I wonder why she is at Highfields. Do you know that Mrs Boase's husband has had to raise another mortgage on their house to keep his wife there, because of you? And Mr Deansborough can walk without any crutches but he is still kept there. I would like to know why. There must be dozens of cases where patients are kept in for unnecessarily long periods because they are willing to pay.'

Now that Bryony had spoken she was filled with uneasy panic. How could she have said what she did? Why, oh why had she let her temper run away with her? She clasped her hands together to hide their trembling, and stared down at them.

Suddenly she was grasped by the shoulders and lifted to her feet.

'How . . . dare . . . you . . . speak to me in such a fashion?'

His eyes, like flames now, burnt her with their fury. When he released her she flopped back on to her chair like a discarded rag doll. Tomorrow, she believed her shoulders would be black and blue. He walked to the window and gazed out for a moment or two, then came back to his desk. He sat down and picking up his pen scribbled on a pad. She looked miserably to see what he was writing and to her amazement saw that he was sketching her. She recognised the collar of her dress, her hair, the shape of her face. She wondered what was going to happen next. If she stood up she was certain she would fall down.

At last he said in a carefully controlled voice,

'You lost your temper and that is always unwise, one is apt to say and do things that are later regretted. So I would like you to take time to cool down. Will you promise me not to do anything about it for the time being?'

She had a tremendous feeling of reprieve. 'Yes,' she whispered.

'Thank you. And, my dear, you really must try to control your temper.'

He followed her into the hall. The receptionist had left but the door which led to the rest of the house suddenly opened.

Wendy, wearing a minute jump-suit and with her hair still tied up with the blue ribbon, ran towards them. She slipped her hand in Bryony's, then went across and tugged Dr Crosland's sleeve. She tipped her head back so that she could look into his face.

'Did she say yes, Uncle Ellis?'

'Wendy! To whom are you referring?' He spoke clearly and precisely.

She refused to be downcast but turned eagerly to Bryony.

'You did say you would, didn't you?'

'Would what, Wendy?' Bryony asked.

Wendy turned again to Ellis. 'You did ask her to marry you, didn't you, Uncle? I hope you did. I don't want to have to apologise to Dr Browne.' She pouted and dug her toe into the silky carpet.

Ellis smothered an exclamation. 'I will deal with you later,' he said sternly. 'Run away now. At once.'

She moved slowly and reluctantly to the door and called over her shoulder,

'*Did* you?'

'Wendy!' he thundered, and she disappeared quickly through the door.

He looked at Bryony with an unfathomable expression in his eyes. She turned aside to hide her flaming cheeks.

He put out his hand and lightly touched her face with fingers that made her feel she had been scalded.

'I must apologise for Wendy's behaviour, she is quite impossible.'

'It's quite all right,' Bryony murmured.

His eyes sparkled. 'This meeting has not been a hundred per cent successful, has it?' he said whimsically.

And Bryony hurried out and down the steps and wished with all her heart that she could blot out the sound of amusement in his voice.

CHAPTER TWELVE

BRYONY was sitting alone in the canteen and for once she hoped that Rene would not join her. She had been so apprehensive and preoccupied with the prospect of her interview with Ellis that everything else had been pushed into the background of her mind. Even the fact that Nick had come back.

Last night she had felt no reaction to that, neither happiness, sorrow, nostalgia nor anger. She wondered whether that could have been due to the shock and surprise of seeing him again so unexpectedly. So now she tested her feelings cautiously as she tried to remember the good times and the love they had shared. But it was as if a part of her had died.

He had tossed her love aside when he jilted her, and killed that love. A line from a poem by Shakespeare infiltrated her mind. *Love is not love which alters when it alteration finds*.

Was that true? Hadn't she truly loved him? Perhaps she was not capable of real love. Immediately she discarded that thought. She felt certain that no matter what Ellis did or said, even those things which she disapproved could not quench the overwhelming love she felt for him, the longing just to glimpse him in passing, the need to know that he was somewhere nearby. She yearned to hear his low, authoritative voice, to see the way he moved and the gentle interest in his lovely tawny eyes when he was listening. Oh yes, she knew full well that she could love deeply, even though that love was unrequited.

She had believed that she loved Nick. It was not until she had met Ellis that she knew the meaning of real love. When Ellis touched her, even in anger, it was an experience that she would not have missed. Had he wished to be her lover she knew that she could not have resisted him.

She felt in a strait-jacket of embarrassment at the memory of Wendy's tactless questions. She was a dear little girl and Bryony was fond of her. But how could she ever recover from the humiliation of hearing the amusement in Ellis' voice? No wonder he found it funny, it was a natural reaction, Wendy's suggestion that he should ask her to marry him was indeed preposterous. If only she had not loved him so deeply she could have laughed too, made a joke of it and tossed the remarks aside as the childish nonsense they were. But she was unable to do or say anything but stand petrified and scarlet-faced. That had amused him too, and he made no secret of it. 'I hate him,' she groaned through clenched teeth. 'Hate him, hate him, hate him!' But how could she hate him when she loved him so?

She could still feel the bruising grip of his hands on her shoulders and she was glad, for she could almost pretend that he was here beside her. She was surprised that he had let her off so lightly, for in her professional capacity as a nurse she had contravened all rules, every nicety of protocol in speaking to him as she did. And as a lay person she had been grossly impertinent and rude and she was ashamed. He had been remarkably forbearing after that one short burst of anger and she wished desperately that she had not said the things she had. But words once spoken cannot be recalled, she thought sadly. Her quick temper had caused her much unhappiness in the past and she still had not learned to curb it.

Dr Browne, she had to admit, would make him an ideal wife. Her medical training would mean they could discuss matters on the same level. Her standing in the circle in which they mixed was high, everybody said that she was clever, if not brilliant. She was also striking looking with her slim figure and auburn hair and she dressed well, unlike many of her colleagues. It was quite clear, too, that she was more than willing to become Mrs Crosland, it was hardly likely that she would have told Wendy she was going to marry him unless she had some very good reason for believing it to be so. She thought of Wendy's dislike of Dr Browne and wondered what had prompted it. But children were strange and did not always need to have a reason for their likes and dislikes. Why, for example, had she taken such a fancy to herself? Surely it was not the gift of a blue ribbon that had won her over?

There was still the problem of Mrs Trengwainton

and the thought of another interview with Ellis. That would be sure to lead to further arguments for he had not seemed to take her decision to leave Highfields seriously and she would need to convince him otherwise.

'Hi!'

Rene, bearing a tray laden with roast pork and vegetables, fruit tart and cream, came up beside her.

'Rene!' Bryony covered her eyes with her hands. 'How can you face all that fattening food?'

'My tummy's used to it, that's how.'

She transferred her dishes to the table. 'Have you heard about Nurse Middleton?'

'Nurse Middleton? I don't think I know her. Why? What has she done?'

'She's on the staff at Polwithy. You must have seen her at the dance—oh well, perhaps you didn't. Anyhow, she was in a car crash a couple of nights ago, poor soul.'

'Was she badly hurt?'

'Yes, she is in intensive care at Polwithy. She's injured her back, and they doubt if she will be able to carry on nursing. It's fatal to have a bad back in our game. Shame. I like Mavis, she's always a lot of fun.'

'Rotten luck. But I suppose it's a blessing she wasn't killed. Maybe it won't be as bad as they fear.'

'I hope not. You know, it seemed horrible. I went over to see her and already they were talking of getting a replacement for her. I know it makes sense because they can't afford to be short-staffed. But it made me shiver.'

'I know what you mean. It's like saying, "The King is dead. Long live the King".'

'Exactly.' Rene ate in silence for a few minutes, then she said thoughtfully, 'I was almost tempted to apply for the job myself. Then I thought of all this luxury and super food and decided against it.'

A startled look of awareness came into Bryony's eyes. If only *she* could get the job. She would be able to move from Highfields with its private medicine and extortionate fees without the alternative of going to work for Mrs Trengwainton which, in her innermost heart, she knew she would not like.

'You've given me an idea, Rene. I think I'll try for that.'

'You think you'd like it better than here?'

Bryony nodded. 'I think I would. I don't really approve of private nursing homes and the very high fees the patients have to pay. I know it wouldn't be anything like as comfortable as here but I did apply there in the first place when there were no vacancies.'

'In that case I should nip over there right away before they put out the advert. Ask to see the Chief Nursing Officer. And good luck.' Rene gave her a cheery grin.

Bryony hesitated. 'You—you don't think it will look callous with poor Nurse Middleton lying there—'

'No, not at all. They need a nurse and you want the job. That's fair enough.'

Bryony gave her a grateful smile. 'Thanks Rene. Mind you, if I get it I'll miss you a lot.'

'Yes, I'm a fool to myself telling you about it. Still, that's life.'

Entering Polwithy General hospital seemed almost as familiar to Bryony as going into St Stephen's. There were the same long, wide corridors, the pale green distempered walls, the hospital smells, the sound of footsteps and trolleys and the metallic clatter of bed-pans in distant sluices. No sound was muted by curtains or carpets as at Highfields. But Bryony felt an inner warm glow, an excitement as of coming home after being a long time away.

Sign-posts pointed in all directions. To the Path lab, ear, throat and nose clinic, X-ray department, lecture rooms, etcetera. Bryony looked around her, uncertain which direction to take. A pretty West Indian nurse paused and asked her with a pleasant smile if she could help.

'Yes, please. I want the Chief Nursing Officer's room.'

'You go to the end of this corridor and turn to the left. You will see it written up on the door.'

Bryony thanked her and followed her directions, then tapped on the door marked Miss B. Tonkin.

'Enter,' a disembodied voice replied.

She was a small middle-aged woman who raised her brows on seeing Bryony.

'Who are you?'

'Nurse Sellers, ma'am. From Highfields Nursing Home. Thank you for seeing me.'

'Hm! I don't seem to have been given any option.'

'I'm sorry, I know that I should have made an appointment, but I wanted to speak to you urgently if I may.'

Miss Tonkin frowned. 'This is most unusual. What is it that you wanted to see me about?'

'It's about the vacancy that I believe you have, ma'am.'

'Vacancy?' she snapped. 'What do you know about a vacancy?'

'I—I heard the sad news about Nurse Middleton and that her position would have to be filled, and I would very much like to be considered for it.'

'I see. But you are working at Highfields?'

'Yes. Only because I couldn't get in here.'

Miss Tonkin's eyes wandered slowly over her. 'I understand it is very comfortable at Highfields. Why do you wish to leave?'

Bryony hesitated. She wondered what Miss Tonkin's reaction would be if she told the truth and said that she could not bear to work under Dr Crosland because she was not sure whether she loved him or hated him. That would certainly be the surest way of losing both jobs.

'I am happy there, ma'am, but I prefer NHS work. I did write to you here before I took the post at Highfields, but there was no vacancy.'

'I see. Well, I should need to see your reports and references from—where did you do your training?'

'At St Stephen's in London.'

'Oh, St Stephen's.' Her change of voice showed the regard she had for that hospital. 'And I will want to know Dr Crosland's opinion of your work at Highfields.'

Colour flooded Bryony's cheeks. She had overlooked the fact that a reference would be required from him.

'Yes ma'am, I can let you see those from St Stephen's immediately. Do you want me to ask Dr Crosland for one?'

'You can leave that to me. If your application is successful you would start on night duty. I take it you are fully trained?'

'Yes ma'am. I have my SRN.'

'Good. Then if you will let me have the references.'

'Straight away, ma'am.'

Miss Tonkin nodded and gave her a pleasant smile of dismissal.

When at last Bryony knew that she had been given the vacancy she felt a tremendous relief. She would be away from the strain of seeing and hopelessly loving Ellis despite the fact that he was making so much money from sick people. She would be away from the cloying atmosphere of too much luxurious living and would be doing something which she knew was worthwhile, something for which she had been trained.

Saying goodbye to Rene and Sister Mailer and some of the patients gave her a feeling of sadness but it was only momentary for she would still be working in the vicinity and able to call in on them at any time. Telling Mrs Trengwainton of her plans had been easier than she anticipated.

'I have considered your very generous offer, Mrs Trengwainton, but I must tell you that I have decided to work at Polwithy General—that is the work I enjoy,' Bryony said, in a well-rehearsed speech.

Instead of the display of anger she had feared, Mrs Trengwainton gave her a frosty smile.

'Then we are both well pleased. I hope you will be happy at Polwithy hospital if that is the sort of place you feel at home in. As for me, dear Dr Crosland has put me in touch with a very charming lady whom he considers would be a more satisfactory companion for me than you. And of course I will go along with what he says because he has always had my welfare at heart.'

Bryony had managed to control her feelings while she was with Mrs Trengwainton but when she left her room her anger exploded. How dared he! How dared he take away her chance of a job which, for all he knew, she may have wanted very badly? With a car and her salary doubled anyone might have jumped at it, yet he had the audacity to infer that she was not suitable! The fact that she did not

want it was neither here nor there. What right had he to spoil her chances? Thank goodness she would no longer be working under him!

The lights of Polwithy hospital were dimmed. Night Sister Wilcox and Bryony accompanied the Sister who was going off duty on her rounds.

'Mrs Green has two hourly Heparin to retard blood clotting. Dr Russell knows about this but if he is held up bleep Dr Wayne. The next injection is due at one-thirty,' Sister said in a hoarse whisper indicating a patient who had butterfly needles in the backs of her hands.

They paused momentarily at each bed. 'Mrs Gibbs needs to pass water frequently. She can make her own way to the toilet but occasionally gets a dizzy spell so watch out for that.'

They came to a patient with a drip and all three of them looked up at it automatically.

'In another hour or so that will need replacing. Saline and glucose, it's in her notes. Mrs Reynolds is a suspect duodenal and needs a warm drink at three o'clock usually. Only if she asks. No one else needs one but they'll try to get it if they can, I daresay. Three ops tomorrow. The notices are over the beds. I think that's all. So I'll wish you a quiet night.' She put on her cloak and walked swiftly down the corridor.

'It's a little unfair to leave you here on your own on your first night but we are very understaffed. I am in charge of all the wards so I am afraid you won't be seeing much of me,' Sister Wilcox said.

Bryony's heart fell. Never had she felt more vulnerable.

'In an emergency, who can I contact, Sister?'

'Come and I'll show you.' She led the way into the office and pointed to a list of dates and phone numbers pinned on the wall. 'Ring this number if you need help but I need hardly remind you that you are a qualified nurse and will not make a frivolous call.'

'No Sister,' Bryony said forlornly.

'Our nights are usually quiet so you should have nothing to worry about. Take away the water on the lockers at midnight, where it says "Nil by mouth", and make sure the patients do not have morning tea or breakfast. Is there anything you want to ask me?' She turned over the watch which was pinned on to her apron and stood ready to leave.

'I can't think of anything at the moment, Sister.'

'I will send along a junior if I can find one who can be spared.'

'Thank you Sister, that would be good.'

When Sister Wilcox had left, Bryony walked around the ward again to familiarise herself with the patients' names and conditions. Snores filled the ward with unbelievable loudness and patients in nearby beds moved restlessly and coughed in protest. Here and there a patient stared at her with wide open unblinking eyes, unable to sleep but knowing that it was useless to complain. Bryony checked that a replacement drip lay in readiness and that the one in use was still functioning properly. Then she settled down at the table at the end of the ward and glanced at some medical journals.

She was glad to be here and thought yet again how much she preferred this atmosphere to that at Highfields. Here all basic needs were catered for and every attention given to those who were in need. She felt nauseated at the memory of the scented air, the luxurious fittings and the expensive food at Highfields. But more than that she disliked the domineering attitude of some of the patients, their belief that money could buy them the best attention and treatment and could even delay, if not completely prevent, their departure to the next world.

Momentarily her thoughts went to Ellis. He had everything, good looks, status, impeccable taste and money. So why did he expend his talents on people like that? He had no need to do so. Why, oh why couldn't he care for the sick because he wanted to help them? Because then, she answered herself, he would be perfect. And no man was.

The phone rang in the office and she hastened to answer it before it could disturb the patients. The call was from Casualty to say that a patient with suspected appendicitis was being admitted.

Bryony prepared a bed and switched on the electric blanket. Soon a trolley rattled along the corridor and voices sounded, loud enough to wake every patient in the ward but they slept on, thanks to their sleeping pills. When the patient was transferred to the bed the porter handed Bryony her notes.

'Doctor will be up in a few minutes,' he said, and trundled the trolley away.

The words had hardly faded when the lift doors opened and someone stepped out and paused at the door. Bryony hurried across and came face to face with Ellis Crosland.

'You!' she said, the word escaping from her. Then the colour flooded her cheeks at her effrontery.

'Nurse Sellers! Hello, how are you?'

Without waiting for a reply he strode across to the new patient, asked Bryony to draw the curtains around the bed, then took the girl's hands in his.

'Well now, my dear, you didn't expect to be in here tonight, I'll wager, Miss—?'

'Appleby,' the girl said and looked at him with scared, pain-filled eyes.

He sat on the edge of her bed and asked Bryony for her notes.

'Ah yes. Miss Joan Appleby. Do you mind if I call you Joan?'

'No. Please do,' she said weakly.

There was silence as he read carefully through her notes. Then he looked at her with warm, friendly eyes.

'Now Joan, tell me everything that happened, will you?'

'I've already told them in Casualty,' she protested.

'Yes, I know that. But I would like to hear what you have to say, Joan.'

When she had finished he gave a brief nod. 'Right. Well I'll just take a look if I may. Nurse—'

Bryony arranged the sheets and exposed the patient's appendix area. His sensitive fingers touched the patient so gently that Bryony marvelled that he could learn anything from that, but he seemed satisfied and motioned to Bryony to cover her up again.

'I'll get Nurse to give you something that will send you to sleep and I'll come and see you again in the morning.'

'Are you—are you going to take my appendix out, Doctor?' the girl asked anxiously.

'Why? Do you want to keep it for any reason?' His lovely honey-gold eyes laughed at her gently.

'Well no—but I . . .'

'But you are not keen on the idea of having it out. I understand. But there is nothing at all to worry about one way or the other. If it has to come out I promise you you will only have a very small scar—nothing to stop you wearing a bikini if we get any summer weather.' He held her hands for a few minutes longer, then with a final reassuring smile he moved away.

Bryony had watched the interchange between them with a swelling heart, he was so charming, so caring, no wonder patients loved him. She had almost envied Joan for the complete interest he had shown her.

Before leaving the ward he went over to Mrs Green's bed and then to the patient with the drip.

'This is due to be replaced, Nurse. And have you checked the time for the Heparin?

Bryony glanced at her watch. 'Dr Russell should be here in a few minutes, sir.'

'Good. No problems with any of the other patients?'

'No sir.'

When they reached the ward doors Ellis paused. 'This is your first time on duty?'

'Yes sir.'

'And do you think that you are going to like it better than Highfields?'

She looked up at him and was filled with a longing which made her body ache for him. If only he were hers there was nothing else in life that she would want. She knew that she loved him more in these last few minutes than in all the time at Highfields, for the caring attention he had shown this patient was real and not because he was being handsomely rewarded.

'Yes, oh yes.'

'Weren't you comfortable there?'

'Very comfortable indeed. But I don't agree with private medicine.' She felt her cheeks burn.

He was about to reply when a young man stepped out of the lift.

'Ah Dr Russell. Good. Then I'll be on my way home.'

The young man seemed flustered. 'I'm sorry I'm a bit late, sir. For the new admission, I mean.'

'That's all right,' Ellis said casually. 'Good-night—or rather good morning.'

He stepped into the lift, pressed the button, then slid out of sight.

As Dr Russell injected the Heparin into the butterfly needles the patient gave a quiet moan.

'It does make my hands ache, Doctor.'

'But it's necessary, Mrs Green, and I don't suppose it will be for much longer.'

'You're new, aren't you?' he said to Bryony as they walked away.

'Yes, my first time on duty here.'

'What is the new admission?'

'Appendix. I think she must be pretty bad because Dr Crosland came to see her immediately.'

'That doesn't signify. Dr Crosland insists that he is told of any admission during the night and invariably comes to see the patient.'

'But I thought there was a list of doctors on duty?'

'There is and I am on call tonight. I wasn't very late in coming but even so, he was here first. He never says anything, no matter how late we are—occasionally someone oversleeps—he just makes us feel really guilty to think that he has made the effort to come and we haven't.'

'He must work very hard with the nursing home

patients to attend to as well,' Bryony said thoughtfully.

'Yes, he's an exceptional man. And he treats every patient as if they are the most important one on his list. I don't think he cares a damn if they are private or NHS but he seems to have a soft spot for the patients in here. Well cheers, and a quiet night—what's left of it.'

When Bryony had attended to the needs of her patients she went back to her seat at the table. How stupid she had been condemning Ellis for faults she just imagined that he had. How cruel and how rude. Ever since she had first heard his name mentioned she had misjudged him and she knew it was because of the way Nick had behaved. If only she could take back the things she had said. But it was too late.

Grey morning light began to show in the ward. An occasional lorry, heavily laden with waste from the Newlyn quarries, on its way to Castle-an-dinas rumbled along the street and shook the windows. There was the sound of increased activity in the hospital as ancillary workers came on duty. Soon another day would have begun.

CHAPTER THIRTEEN

BRYONY had almost reached Harbour View when a car zoomed alongside her. Ellis called out,

'Can you spare me a few moments, Nurse?'

She stopped and hesitated. This had all happened before. On the day she arrived at Polwithy. Then too he had invited her into his car and she had been reluctant to accept. But, as on that occasion, she climbed into the seat beside him.

'I was just going home,' she said.

'But you are not in a hurry?'

'No.'

He put his foot on the accelerator and they moved off.

'Oh—I thought you just wanted to speak to me. Where are you going?'

'I am taking you to a place that I think you will like. To my mind it is the prettiest place in Cornwall.'

As he drove through the narrow lanes and around hairpin bends and up and down steep hills she looked at his slim hands on the steering-wheel and felt an unbearable longing to touch them, to feel his tanned cheek against hers and to run her fingers through his hair. She clenched her hands together in her lap.

He slowed the car to a crawl as they turned a corner and came to a wooded and flower-strewn valley where a trout stream ran like a silver ribbon down to the sea, and a sandy cove, flanked by lichen-covered cliffs, sparkled in the sunlight.

'Oh Ellis!' Bryony breathed, unaware that she had said his name. 'This must be the most beautiful place in the world.

He looked pleased. 'I thought you would like it. Shall we sit outside for a while?'

He parked the car and they stepped out on to springy emerald turf where thrift grew in massive pink clumps. The air was scented with wild flowers and the only sounds were of running, singing water and the cry of birds. They sat side by side with rocks from an outcrop as back-rests.

'I brought you here so that we would be free from interruptions. There is so much I want to say to you, Bryony.'

She looked at him questioningly.

'But first of all I want you to tell me about your past. I want to know what hurt you so much.'

His eyes were smoky-gold as he gazed down at her. She shook her head. 'No—please—I'd rather not talk about it.'

His voice was gently persuasive. 'I want to know, Bryony.'

'No,' she said again. 'It's all over now and I would rather forget.'

He touched her hand. 'Please Bryony?'

She hated to admit that she had once been jilted.

'You wouldn't understand,' she said.

'Try me,' he persisted.

There was something about him and despite herself she found she was telling him all about Nick. About the happiness and then his rejection and the misery and disillusionment. And then of his return which was even more shaming. It all came tumbling out.

Ellis leaned back on his folded arms, his eyes screwed up against the sun. They sat in silence when she had finished. Bryony felt drained for this was the first time she had told the details to anyone. Yet in some strange way she felt less bitter.

At last Ellis said softly, 'Thank you for telling me, Bryony, for now I can understand why you imagined that I was motivated by the thought of making money. But, my dear, you cannot judge the whole world by one man.'

His nearness made her tremble. 'I know that now. I realised how wrong I was about you when I went to work at Polwithy. I had thought that you treated the patients with so much care because they paid for their treatment. Now I know that isn't true. And I am deeply sorry for the awful things I said to you. I know you can never forgive me, I can't forgive myself.'

'But I can understand your feelings, so I think it is only fair to speak on my own behalf, and explain . . .'

'No please—I don't want you to explain—not now,' she protested.

'But I must. Today you are satisfied, but on another occasion when for some reason you might not feel so kindly disposed towards me, you could feel differently. And I don't want that to happen. So please listen to me. I believe you feel that the charges at Highfields are too high?'

'Well—you can't deny that.'

'I don't. But have you considered the cost of running it? It is a nursing home for wealthy people because there is a need for such a place down here. They would get precisely the same medical treatment at Polwithy, but without the frills. But these patients *want* the frills, they have the money and are willing to pay for them. As you know, they have individual attention from the nurses which means that I have to employ a large staff on high salaries. I have a *cordon bleu* chef in the kitchen to provide them with the kind of food they enjoy and are accustomed to. Don't imagine we make a fortune from Highfields because we don't.'

'Yes, I understand,' Bryony said thoughtfully. 'But sometimes I have wondered why the patients are kept there even after they seem better.'

'After they seem better to you. But take Winston Deansborough, for example. His is a rare condition and I have to be satisfied that he is well enough to be discharged and that the trouble will not flare up again, or all his expensive treatment would be wasted. Had he been in Polwithy his bed would undoubtedly have been needed, and as his records would show that he seemed fit to leave that is what he would have had to do because we have to make the best use of the facilities there. At Highfields I can keep him in that much longer.'

Bryony felt ashamed that he was giving her such careful explanations and of her previous suspicions. Then she remembered Mrs Trengwainton.

'But what about Mrs Trengwainton? You told me yourself that there was nothing wrong with her and yet she had been with you for ages.'

He broke off a stem of purple heather and threaded it in her buttonhole.

'Ah yes, Mrs Trengwainton. She is a lonely woman and has nobody at home but her staff. They look after her house well enough, but she craves personal attention. When I admitted her she was not ill enough to have occupied a bed in hospital but in my opinion she was on the verge of a breakdown through nothing but loneliness. Here we provide company and pamper her. Sometimes a person needs to be spoiled a little. We act as a crutch until the patient is mentally as well as physically strong enough to cope on her own. Sometimes it takes a long time. It would be pointless to discharge her too soon.'

Bryony was silent for a moment. 'So she needs a companion. But you gave her the name of someone you said would be more suitable to be with her than me. Why did you do that? Have you such a poor opinion of me?' she asked reproachfully.

His eyes flickered. 'I was thinking of you as much as of her. It would be the wrong life for you.'

'But she needed me, she told me so.'

'She needed somebody—but not necessarily you. Everybody needs somebody.' After a moment he added softly, 'It is I who need you.'

Her eyes opened wide. 'You need me?'

'Every day I look out for a golden-haired girl whose very presence does the strangest things to me. What would I do if you went away?'

The tenderness in his eyes was so overwhelming that it sent a tremor through her whole body. She lowered her lashes to hide from him the love which she knew must be shining in her eyes.

He whispered, 'Marry me, Bryony.'

'Wh-what did you say?'

'Sweet Bryony, will you marry me?'

Heaven was inviting her but a shadow fell across her face as once more she remembered.

'No—please Ellis—I couldn't bear it to happen again. I still have nothing to offer . . .'

His mouth was firmly over hers in a kiss that was tender yet passionate and it was as if she had waited all her life for this moment. But she knew what she had to say. She struggled to move away from him.

'I'm not rich or clever . . .'

He looked at her with a wicked smile. 'I know that, my darling. But think how pleased Wendy would be. She wouldn't have to apologise to Thea!'

A pained look came into her eyes. 'Thea? Oh Ellis, everybody thinks that you and Thea—' She could say no more.

He kissed the eyes that looked up at him so sadly.

'I loved you the very first time I met you. I will never forget that day, you were so pretty, so shy, so excited, so unconsciously saying all the wrong things. That is when I fell in love with you.'

'Did you really, Ellis? I loved you too. I couldn't get you out of my mind. I still can't,' she admitted shyly.

'You haven't answered my question,' he reminded her.

'And you haven't answered mine. About Thea '

'Thea has been my friend and colleague for a number of years, we are excellent working partners. Had I wanted to marry her I should have asked her long ago. But the only girl I ever wanted to be my wife is you. Must I ask you again?'

She looked at him with shy adoration. 'Yes please, Ellis. Ask me again. It is the loveliest thing I have ever heard and once is not enough.'

'Shylock!' he said, kissing the tip of her nose. 'Bryony, sweet Bryony, will you be my wife?'

'Yes, oh yes,' she breathed.

The sun, a flaming ball of fire, streaked the sky with scarlet and filled the valley with a pink glow which surrounded them, but they only had eyes for each other.

Seagulls circling overhead swooped low to take a closer look, then, screeching their delight, flew noisily out to sea.

Mills & Boon
Happy Mother's Day
-with love
Mills & Boon